What People Are Saying About

You Complete the Masterpiece

Perceptive and intimate, you will want to savour every line in this timely book. Mankowski takes me into the world of this novel with such sensitivity, his writing is so poised it's a pleasure to read. Reminded me of The Talented Mr Ripley.
Ruth Dugdall, bestselling author of *My Sister and Other Liars* and the Cate Austin series

It's unusual to find a young male writer who can write with such sensitivity and maturity. This is clearly a writer of great talent. Already recognised as a major rising talent, Mankowski has established himself as a significant voice in British fiction.
Andrew Crumey, Man Booker longlisted author of *Sputnik Caledonia*

I'd read another Mankowski in a flash, because I like his writing so much.
Marsha Skrypuch, Our Choice Award-winning author

T0284318

You Complete the Masterpiece

A Novel

You Complete the Masterpiece

A Novel

Guy Mankowski

ROUNDFIRE BOOKS

London, UK
Washington, DC, USA

CollectiveInk

First published by Roundfire Books, 2024
Roundfire Books is an imprint of Collective Ink Ltd.,
Unit 11, Shepperton House, 89 Shepperton Road, London, N1 3DF
office@collectiveink.com
www.collectiveink.com
www.roundfire-books.com

For distributor details and how to order please visit the 'Ordering' section on our website.

Text copyright: Guy Mankowski 2023

ISBN: 978 1 80341 661 8
978 1 80341 660 1 (ebook)
Library of Congress Control Number: 2023945507

A CIP catalogue record for this book is available from the British Library.

Design: Lapiz Digital Services

UK: Printed and bound by CPI Group (UK) Ltd, Croydon, CR0 4YY
Printed in North America by CPI GPS partners

We operate a distinctive and ethical publishing philosophy in all areas of our business, from our global network of authors to production and worldwide distribution.

Also by Guy Mankowski

The Intimates (Legend Press, 2011) ISBN-10: 1907756469
Letters from Yelena (Legend Press, 2012) ISBN-10: 1909039101
How I Left the National Grid (Roundfire, 2014) ISBN-10: 178279896X
An Honest Deceit (Urbane Publications, 2015) ISBN-10: 191112997X
"Dead Rock Stars" (Darkstroke, 2020) ISBN 9798667780991
Albion's Secret History: Snapshots of England's Pop Rebels and Outsiders (Zero Books, 2021) ISBN 978-1-78904-028-9

This book is dedicated to Shirley Firmin, with love.

Acknowledgements

Thanks to the staff at 200 Degrees, Lincoln. Thank you Nikita Fellows for early edits, and for the crowd at New Art Social, Newcastle for their feedback on early drafts; a great crowd of gifted creatives. I'm grateful to John Romans for his perceptive editing. Thanks to everyone at 'The Gingers Fingers'. I would like to offer my loving thanks to Lou Woodcock, my family and lastly to Rachel Butler.

Part One

1

The story doesn't start with the manuscript, or how it reassembled my life. For me, the story starts at five in the morning on my second day in Barcelona. I'm lying in the rich, crisp Egyptian sheets in the Barcelona flat the award committee have deemed my home for the next four weeks. But it is not the email I received two weeks before – telling me my last novel has won a major award – that is keeping me awake. Nor the tyranny of my body, which demands my scratches and twitches, or a mind which refuses to clear for ten straight seconds, instead dredging up the detritus of past shame and current anxiety. It is instead the need to relive, one mental step at a time, a lost mood from my childhood. I am lying in the sheets trying to isolate and define that mood, because at that moment in my life I am terrified. Despite the fact that this award has lifted me out of debt and obscurity, taking me from the heavy skies of England to the bright tapestries of Mediterranean horizons, I am terrified because I no longer know who I am. I am lying there, trying to remember how I was as a child. I am trying to stay sane.

The first thought I have, as I close my eyes, is the memory from my childhood home. In early mornings there, before anyone woke up, I was aware of the sanctity of waking up in a house a few yards from the sea. I felt grateful to live on a sunlit street full of brittle early morning light. It seemed to possess a quality which lit the curtains in a warm glow, bathing me. In these childhood thoughts I would think of the driveways outside the houses in the street. The inhabitants were sleeping and I thought of their comfortable problems and their vague aspirations. I thought of the dew lit by the dawn, illuminating the lawns so they looked like beds of diamonds. I would hear the early morning cry of an owl, nestled in some invisible tree.

I would dream of one day getting up early and seeing the night turn into day over a calm ocean. Seeing the world I knew come to life; witnessing its moment of inception. I would trace the imperceptible moment darkness became light. All those thoughts would lull me into a state of security. All I knew at that age was to cherish that state of mind. Secure as it seemed, there was an abstract luminescence in the sensation these surroundings inspired, and inarticulate as I was I sensed the impermanence. I realised even then that the existence of these rich surroundings was temporary, and that at some point in the future I would come to miss it. Lying in the sheets in Barcelona, that time has come.

I know that when the day begins I won't be able to talk of these thoughts. Not even to the students who want to hear me talk about my writing. Even though they have ostensibly come to hear me talk about my last novel – and the man who influenced it – I know that they do not really want real insight from me. They do not want to hear that my need to be a writer started with those childish imaginings, inspired as they were by a need to step outside of routine life. They do not even want to hear about the inherent absurdity of a writer now being deemed worthy of sharing his thoughts at ticketed events, when only a few weeks ago he was treated as an irrelevance. My five a.m. thoughts now are barely palpable for me, in the context in which I live. I have only shared them with Francine, and that was during the first conversation we had, where whisky and insomnia made our thoughts swirl. I don't know why she understood them and why she alone was able to offer insights that made me feel sane. But regardless, these students will just want to hear about how I struggled to write a novel. They will look up, with blank and shining faces, wanting me to reflect their own frustrations and rejections. When you start being successful you become like a mirror. People think they are seeing themselves in you but there are all kinds of mirrors, and the best ones are beautiful themselves. These students want me to validate them, when I am yet to validate myself.

Why was I chosen for this award? Was it a trick?

As I flip over in the sheets I remember the one consoling thought I have. The fact that the one writer who captured these five a.m. thoughts bequeathed me this award. Alberto Valdez. The only author I've ever read that captured the jagged and sensual nature of this shifting life. It was the strange rhythms of his writing, with its hidden messages and rich, ornate symbolism that first made me believe I could capture my mind on the page. It was his own granddaughter, Maria, who had emailed to tell me Valdez had wanted me to be the first author given the award in his name. The news of his presumed death, six months before that email, had removed a sense of belonging I had in the world. I had known for a few years that he was struggling with his mental health, but hearing that his car had been left on a renowned suicide spot had marked my life with an emotional full stop. I remember where I was when I heard David Bowie had died, I remember where I was when I heard Leonard Cohen had died, and I remember where I was when I heard Alberto Valdez was gone. The email from Maria meant so much to me it was almost absurd – but until I heard from my publisher that the prize was real I had felt unable to celebrate.

This ennobling confirmed not only that Valdez had taken a liking to my last book, but that it was the *only* book he had felt able to honour with his award. It was strange to know that a trophy sharing our names would one day sit on a bedside table in my house, a home filled with volumes of his surrealist stories.

Since that sacred email I have started getting replies from my publisher and agent, as well as daily messages from strangers. They all now write in the warm tones of the familial. Their sudden change of tone, with its defiant lack of self-awareness, is perhaps what has prompted my early morning panics. During these panics I go over the details about my stay here.

Following the 8000 Euros I received on agreeing to the terms of the award, I will attend an award ceremony at the university here. At the end of the trip I will give a talk to the students, which will conclude with yet another 8000 Euros being awarded to me. In the interim I will deal with whatever interviews and photo-shoots I am offered. These will be interviews given mostly by journalists keen to exploit Valdez's name, or by those intrigued by the unprecedented nature of this award. I will then return home rejuvenated. I will then finish my next book and live the life of an author.

When I think through these details, cracks and sores in my psyche are healed and smoothed. Right now I am not only an author in name, but in lifestyle. The first cheque paid off my monstrous debts, built as a result of meagre royalties earned to date. The second cheque will allow me a few months to get on my way – and publicity from the award should keep me on track. My days of busking to pay the gas bill are, I hope, now behind me.

I remember my arrival at Barcelona airport. In the longest email my agent had yet sent she explained how Maria would meet me at Arrivals. As I wheeled my suitcase to the exit I had not pictured Maria would be a dark-eyed young woman evoking an oil painting by Daeni.

As I fixed upon the woman holding up my name on a card I realised she had the full red lips and thick dark hair of one of his muses – if they had been invigorated by a relentless procession of Spanish summers. Her piercing eyes recalled the image of Valdez in the flap of *Marble*. But the rest of his slanted face, with his mischievous smile and distant hairline, was not apparent in her striking looks.

She recognised me with a smile that was sudden and childlike. 'Jude?' she asked. I nodded.

'I am parked just outside,' she said, her words holding a light Spanish lilt.

As she placed my suitcase in the front of her red sports car I wondered when the gods had begun smiling on me. Her slim, bronze figure was encased in a fitted black dress, cut off below her shoulders. The thick dark hair, swept back over her head, teased the tips of her shoulders. She seemed either unaware, or dismissive, of the effect she had on me.

As she drove, the shimmering heat obscured vibrant adverts on the horizon. Chanel and gasoline mingled in the air as I gathered my thoughts.

'I'm so glad you accepted this award,' she said, looking right for traffic at a junction. Her voice was clear and direct over the clean hum of the engine.

I decided her confident English revealed an education in multiple countries. I tried to find fault with the pristine façade of light makeup, the thick red lips and the delicately enunciated eyes. My failure to find a flaw pained me. I was aware that her Mediterranean looks would paralyse me if she held my gaze for more than a few seconds. My hunch was proven right – as she looked for my reaction she rendered me speechless.

'I have to admit – I was relieved, to get it,' I said.

'Relieved?'

I placed my hand on the roof of the car as it eased into motion. 'Yes. I mean, why wouldn't I accept it? 16,000 Euros and a month in a Spanish apartment. With me being only required to give a lecture and attend a ceremony in return.'

She looked over, bemused.

'And for you to finish off my grandfather's last collection,' she said, lowering her gaze onto me.

2

For a moment I wondered if I was at the whim of some cosmic joke. A joke that had lulled me into thinking I had left obscurity behind, only for it to be replaced with absurdity.

'What do you mean?' I asked.

'You must have read the contract for the award, before you signed it?'

I mentally thanked Francine for insisting on getting the contract translated before I signed it. As usual, she had been the only one to ask searching questions about a sudden opportunity – others had either shown naked envy or dismissed it with revealing pointedness.

'Of course,' I said, scanning my memory. 'It said something about me looking over a collection he left behind before it's published—'

Panic flashed across her deep green eyes. 'Overlooking, not looking over,' she said, her accent now imposing itself.

'I overlook his final collection?'

'Well, it won't get published if you don't,' she said, her voice rising over the sound of the engine. She gripped the steering will and I saw her knuckles whiten. 'My grandfather's will was very clear. *The recipient of the first award in his name offers their consent over the contents of the collection before it can be released.*' Her swaying head suggested she was calming herself. 'I asked Marco to make this clear to you. How can I be surprised he didn't?' she murmured, to herself.

'Who's Marco?'

Despite the seriousness of the sudden reveal, I lamented the disappearance of the sunny personality who had welcomed me moments ago.

'Marco Velasco. The vice-chancellor of the university.'

I had wondered why the university was playing such a role in this award. But between telling people about my sudden success I had not investigated further. There had been so many people I was in a hurry to prove wrong, piled up in my mind like layered trauma. My impatience to address each one underappreciated the density of each component. The pleasure of the acclaim had caused me to smooth over potential administrative snags when they arose.

'So how is a vice-chancellor involved in the collection?'

'I am sorry you weren't told,' she said. 'It seems that was deliberate.' She nodded, and looked at me as we paused at traffic lights. 'Marco was my grandfather's oldest friend. One of the few blessings of my grandfather's long decline was that he had a lot of time to plan for the future. Even if some of his judgement calls were dubious. My grandfather was well aware of the impact of his work. He and I planned the creation of an award in his name many times. With my grandfather having fallen out with most of the family he left the management of his literary estate to his best friend, Marco. He thought even if *I* were involved the family would influence me. My family hated all this, by the way.'

She put on a pair of sunglasses. I caught a scent of perfume, and wondered if she had applied it just before we met.

'Anyway,' she said. 'As my grandfather became more and more isolated Marco got more and more control. He made some controversial decisions. He used my grandfather's royalties to fund some of his own pet projects. I'm talking considerable amounts of money. And yes, he happens to be the vice-chancellor of the university.'

'Who are paying for my award?'

She looked dazed. 'Yes,' she said.

I leant back in the seat.

'And why would they do that?'

She creased her brow. 'I don't know how best to answer that. My grandfather stated in his will that the award be given to you, but on the basis that you decided what parts of his final collection be published.'

'Why me?'

We stopped at traffic lights, and she sleeked her hand through her hair. 'He believed you were the only one that understood his writing,' she said, turning to me with a smile. 'He raved about your last novel – about how so many writers *said* he had influenced them but you were the only one who proved it.'

'It is so strange to hear that. You know, I have a picture of him on my fridge at home? From when he was directing his first play.'

She smiled. 'I know this must be strange. Especially as it is such a surprise.'

But you were the one emailing me, I thought. Who else would I have heard from?

I wracked my brains. Either Francine's translator had done a poor job, or the completion of the collection was scarcely mentioned in the contract.

'You okay?' she asked.

'I still don't get why I have to make the decision on what is included in his last collection. I mean – don't get me wrong. I'm honoured.'

'Good.'

'Valdez was – is – my favourite writer. I wouldn't be here if it wasn't for him, so I feel a sense of duty to him.'

She smiled again. 'Sure.'

'But I just don't remember reading anything about this.'

As we began to move, Maria remained silent. It occurred to me that Velasco might not have wanted this extra requirement of me to be made clear until I had landed in the country. Filling the silence, I said:

'Wouldn't the vice-chancellor – or you – be better equipped to choose the contents of your grandfather's last collection?'

'He was very clear,' she said, looking at me with steady eyes. 'Once he was institutionalised – and as he got sicker – I was the only member of his family he even began to get close to. He said that if anything happened to him he wanted me to work *with* you to decide what is included. But he said it was you who had the final say.'

I laughed. It was a drier sound than I had expected. It didn't reflect my abstract wondering if what other people had called his illness had in fact been some brilliant lucidity on his part. 'It is a lot of pressure; he has to be the most famous Spanish writer of—'

'Yeah, I know,' she said. She'd evidently had a lifetime of hearing that, and praise being heaped on men when she possessed an intellect to more than rival them was something she had no further appetite for. 'I had been trying to work out how to edit the collection to completion before you arrived. To take the pressure off.'

'Well, thank you for that.'

She did not flinch.

'My grandfather knew that getting you to come to Barcelona would be the only way to ensure you could do the job properly. Hence the award.'

Hence me getting half of the money before flying out, in case I back out, I thought.

'Sounds like it might not be a straightforward job,' I said.

'He was sure it could be done in a month. That's the limit he set.'

As I looked at the approaching city – this slippery twist of dusted metal and concrete – it grew more and more blurred. Why had Valdez left so many rules and stipulations behind for a writer he had never met? Why had he left it to his friend – and Maria – to action his will?

'It was good of this vice-chancellor to ensure your grandfather got his final wish,' I said.

Maria didn't say a word. Her face did not move. She took a right, and for a few minutes nosed the sports car down small alleys. We pulled up on the pavement opposite a neon-lit café. The tall building had a gold plaque outside. Its flawless sheen suggested there would be lavish interiors inside.

Maria stayed silent as we entered a faux-marble entrance, lined with bronze statues. We darted up stone staircases. I decided that her body language suggested sudden introspection, rather than anger. She took out a large bunch of keys, and fiddled to open the oak door. As we entered the apartment I inhaled at the sight of the open plan living room – far more modern than the exterior had anticipated. It smelt of flowers and cooling dust. Vast glass windows at my right overlooked a new wooden balcony, and behind it I could see the darkening city. A carnival of flashing lights, faint horns and distant greetings. To my left, a white arch signified the start of a large kitchen area, complete with a new table set.

'I am sure you'll be very happy here,' she said.

There was a faint note of resentment in her voice.

'You mentioned we would be overlooking the collection together,' I said. 'You do know I can't read Spanish?'

She laughed.

'He wrote his last collection in English. Just like his first.' She brushed a strand of hair from her face. 'I think, like Nabokov, he wrote better in English than in his mother tongue.'

'Well, it's a wonderful language,' I said.

'Possibly my favourite,' she answered, smiling. As she put her hand on my elbow I felt weak. The beauty of her features was almost violent. 'I know this is a lot to take in, but I want you to know something. You are a lifesaver,' she said. 'Without you here, this great work of literature would be lost. There was no one else he would entrust it to.'

That's because he was going mad, I thought.

'You are very committed to following your grandfather's last wishes,' I said. 'That's to your credit.'

'Well, the legality of the terms are tight. And Velasco seems determined to follow them to the letter. They were all dictated when my grandfather was deemed of sound mind by a psychiatrist – before he got too ill. When it was beyond dispute he knew what he was doing.' She had an intellect, I told myself, that was indisputably academic; she had considered each possible obstacle and had decided the world was too self-interested to overcome any pragmatic solutions she had to offer.

'I wonder if he thought something was going to happen to him? Or if these plans suggest he was...' I stopped myself.

'What?' she asked.

'That he was planning something,' I said.

She shook her head. 'I don't believe he planned to end his life. I *knew* him. When it came to his work he was always very clear-minded. He knew what he was doing. Trust me.'

'Your grandfather clearly thought you understood him – and that you were the person for the task.'

'And you,' she said. 'I don't have my grandfather's creativity. Perhaps if I did he would have left the task just to me.'

I decided to react before the morose expression forming on her face took hold.

'He obviously thought we would make a good team.'

She nodded. I was glad she had not taken my remark the wrong way. 'He always said I was a fine reader, but then he always left the compliment there.'

'Perhaps we are like Umberto Eco's perfect combination – the poet and the town crier.'

'You are the poet. I am the crier,' she said.

'Well, I look forward to even more pretentious exchanges between us in good time.'

She laughed. It rang throughout the apartment – a pure note that confirmed the place to be paradise. I imagined the two of us savouring glasses of red while poring over manuscripts.

'Well, pretentious exchanges are my forte. I'm doing a PhD in contemporary literature. It's a requirement that we become adept at such things.'

'A PhD in contemporary literature?'

'Yes,' she said. 'I will be more than qualified for the zero hours contract in a mobile phone shop that I inevitably end up with,' she said.

I smiled, but it was horrific that such a joke between two members of the same generation who lived so far apart landed with such ease.

'I think we will learn a lot from each other,' I said.

She looked out at the city. 'I don't doubt it,' she said.

3

Maria rallied herself, and handed me the set of keys from her pocket. I smelt an intoxicating combination of perfume and city smoke in her hair as she leant towards me. 'Let me show you the rest of the place,' she said.

She handed me the bunch of keys. 'You'll only need the gold one,' she said.

I put them on the glass surface of the coffee table. I followed her past the entrance, and at the end of the hallway she swung open the door to the white bedroom.

Through the large windows on the back wall I could see the central plaza of the university. Skirting it were sculptures – smooth white granite shapes and curved metal shavings that towered over passing students. I saw deep-tanned men on skateboards, tops tied around their waists as they slalomed through the plaza. The volume of their stereos was brutal. As I stepped closer I saw bespectacled women reading paperbacks on benches. This was the city, played out like a film across my very own screen. These men, it seemed, had a similar solipsism by which they arranged experience around them.

She opened a door on the left wall, to reveal a marble bathroom.

'It's a little more modern than my postgrad accommodation,' she said.

'So the vice-chancellor didn't sort you out with a flat like this?'

She shook her head with apparent bitterness. 'No, he did not,' she said.

I excused myself to use the bathroom, as she moved back into the living space. In its mirror I saw a version of myself I didn't recognise. My face was redder, gaunter than I had anticipated. 'I'm working with *her*?' I asked myself, in a stage whisper.

I was shocked by the garishness of my face as it moved. I saw my own mouth say the words, 'I can't handle this.' An internal shiver threatened to take control of my body. I took a few deep breaths, and they captured some of the chaos. I forced a wolfish smile onto my face, to clear the visual palette, and moved outside.

I could hear Maria chatting, in a low voice, to another woman in the hallway. I followed the sound, wondering who the other English person in the building might be. I heard Maria use the words 'famous author' and 'very important collection,' and discovered her stood opposite a young blonde woman, with wide blue eyes that ensnared me as I met them.

'This is Kimberley,' Maria said. 'Kimberley-Jude.'

Kimberley offered me a warm smile, and leant against her doorframe in a manner I read as coquettish. The tight-cropped top and shining black jeans exposed midriff honed for the beach. I realised that the adolescent version of me would have fantasied about the company of a woman like her, letting alone her living across the hall. The situation was becoming ridiculous, surreal enough to form the plot of a particularly sexual Valdez novel; the kind that had dated too badly to exist in a new syllabus.

I couldn't quite read the slight hesitancy in Kimberly's 'Nice to meet you'. I watched Maria's smile fall as I said 'You too.'

'Are you working at the university as well?' I asked.

She shook her head, as Maria looked at the floor. 'As if. I'm doing some modelling,' she said, as I tried to place her accent. I decided on South London. 'A mobile phone ad on the beach. Me and ten other girls.' She looked at Maria. 'Hardly high art!'

'Anyone who gets to work in Barcelona for the summer is in a pretty lucky place,' I said.

Her expression brightened. 'You think? I was starting to think I was way too old for this.' She looked shocked by her own confession.

'Maybe we just need new agents,' I said.

Kimberly laughed. I laughed. Maria looked between us again. I thought I saw her exhale a little.

'So we should start work tomorrow, Jude,' Maria said.

'Yes. I'll be interested to see this infamous collection.'

'I'll be interested to see what you make of it. I–I haven't got my head round it yet.'

'Really?'

Kimberly looked between us, her eyes narrowing.

'We're only allowed to use one copy, but I'll lend you it. Also – I think you should attend a lecture at the Creative Writing department in the morning. Get a feel for the university, and then come over to mine. It might give you ideas for your talk!'

'Sounds good.'

'I'll email you directions, then.'

I said goodbye to the two of them and then went back into my flat and closed my door. I leant against it. 'This is my actual life,' I whispered.

That evening I went walking through the city. As I left the confines of the flat I left also the sense of worthiness it imbued in me. Once I stepped outside its boundaries and walked the streets I got a sense of the raw city.

I passed aimless souls, lingering over cups of coffee in cafes, where the lurid photos of dishes had started to fade under the harsh sun. I detected the thin layer of dust that coated the windows of the shop fronts, static and sad in the evening fug. Through open doorways of shops I saw a shopkeeper eyeing a furtive screen at the side of his till. Watching vivid images of life back home as he checked his phone for missives from it. When he saw me he sat up straight, and smoothed his shirt.

I tried not to think about the unspent currencies, existing only in half-formed sentiment, that I had felt when with Maria and Kimberly. As I tried not to think I saw men approach couples, themselves in delicate states of hand-holding, offering them roses. I followed one incident, my mind teeming. The usurper offered compliments to the woman's previously unappreciated beauty in hesitant English. The women accepted the rose, with its comically long stem, and looked touched, before departing. At which the usurper asked for payment, always from the man accompanying her. The man, whose face had recently begun to wear an expression of bland acquiescence, was now affronted. The usurper had brutally exposed whatever state their relationship was in. There was the insinuation that the man did not sufficiently appreciate the company of the woman if he refused, yet the danger he patronised her if he stumped up. I watched a few such incidents, and the usurper was paid in none. I went from admiring his earnest insouciance, to wondering if he was wreaking injury and uncertainty in what had been unformed situations as he went.

I looked ahead at the outdoor dining terraces on the esplanade. I could see young waitresses trying to entice tourists in with sheaves of plastic menus. Between attempts, I watched these girls trail around in circles, waiting for the next punter. They reminded me of caged creatures, treading in slow circles. I felt the acute charisma of one as I drew close. Her smile switched on with the intensity of a halogen bulb. I could see from the boss lingering behind her that her youthful appeal had been identified as a commodity to exploit. But he was impatient to complete the transaction. As I declined her offer he snorted and I felt a pain in my heart. Her cheap makeup crumbled under the harsh light of the outdoor lamp as she smiled her acceptance.

How had the world got to the point where people's uniqueness was just seen as a feature, something to enhance some merchandise? Even expressions of people's uniqueness – such as their art – were now bargaining chips. I started to wonder if I had been lured into a strange trap. I had never before known Spanish contracts, large cheques and expensive flats be thrown into a deal. This happened in high-minded detective novels surely; not in real life. Certainly not in mine.

I pondered this as I kept moving. When had art become something to enhance an experience, rather than the point of the whole experience? When had art become another accessory on the way towards a rich lifestyle, instead of being the goal itself?

I walked a large, jagged circle of the city. Was I now just another feature of this huge mechanism? A failed writer whose basic skills had been noted, and manipulated to ensure more wealth for someone who already had too much? Wasn't this just what was happening everywhere, a mechanism of greed that now extended even into my obscure, creative world?

No one could care how eccentric my circuitous route around the city was. But it felt somehow criminal that the sadness and ache of the city was passing without being mourned. I felt the sense of panic I had had in the bathroom return.

Back at the flat I sat on the lounger on the balcony. I watched, as the sky appeared to have its luminescence sucked from an invisible point beyond the skyline. I closed my ears and heard the screams, cries and wails of the city clenched in its own pain. A metropolis that seemed to be waiting for something; anticipating. As I watched the sunlight fade I thought again of being a child in my bed. Picturing the moment the sunlight would rise above the sea at the end of my street. Was I closer to happiness back then? Wasn't it better to wait in the dark for the sunlight to rise, than to sit up here and watch a city fade?

I realised that it was Valdez, in his novel *Marble*, who had first made me consider such matters. It was his depictions of people, toiling for a lifestyle they would never have, that had set these thoughts in motion. People determined to make their life an immovable, impenetrable entity, beautiful as marble. Only for their life in retrospect to be celebrated for its swirls and mixtures, aspects which they had not controlled but which were seen as theirs.

I considered the irony of the situation that I had found myself in. It was a situation well out of my own control. It looked beautiful from the outside but in fact was hard and uncompromising. As rain started to fall I decided that I would finish Valdez's work. Not just because I needed the pay cheque. But because I wanted more people to consider alternative ways to live. His writing had made me do that; I wanted it to do that for others too. I wanted to do something meaningful that justified the narrative of relative struggle I'd lived so far.

Once it was dark I went inside. As I showered I scrubbed my body, surprised at the ache lingering around my feet.

I lay in the sheets, but despite my exhaustion I was unable to sleep. None of the breathing patterns and meditative techniques I tried allowed me to shut out what I had felt in the city. As midnight passed I felt as if the sounds of the city through the window were mocking me. Each shout was a new aggressor about to invade the flat.

At one point I was sure I could hear a window being forced open; my mind pictured it with enough conviction that it might've been happening. I found myself praying. When I was a boy my parents had made me attend mass with them; in my panic I believed I was cutting through to some nearby entity when I recited the Hail Mary. During it, in Sunday services my father had always placed his hands on my shoulder as if imparting a valuable tool for use in dark moments, later in life. It worked.

I prayed for someone to come along that would make sense of all my disappointment and confusion. It shocked me how clearly the world 'Francine' etched into my mind's eye, in milky, faint writing. She would see the shallowness of the way we were living. She would understand.

But these thoughts were just an overwhelmed mind, feeding back on itself. In moments such as these I can feel the strength of my own mind. It sits there, like a boulder, about to roll forward. I know that at times I cannot control where it goes, but it terrifies me to think that I have no control over its strength.

I don't know if Mary listened. I think she did.

4

I sat at the back of the lecture theatre – having found online the only one that morning that would be in English.

From the far side of the third row I clocked the range of expressions. They held their pliant faces up to the lecturer, like sunflowers to light. At the end of the talk I was intrigued at what questions these faces would produce. Even without understanding the words used I could see they wanted specifics, clarifications. I wondered if it was just the youth today who were so receptive, so keen to learn? Had the deep debts they had developed engendered a curiosity that bordered on the insatiable?

The lecture was drawing to a close when I heard the soft puff of the door closing. A female form leant against the other side of the seating stack. I did a double take as I realised it was Francine.

My first reaction was one of utter relief. There was now someone in the country that understood how I felt. Who could help me navigate this situation.

Her smile, as she met my eye, held mischief. Francine had made only a vague hint that she would come to Barcelona. There was always a subtle, unhinged air about the way her lips curled. Yet the sheer intensity of her green eyes was mesmerising enough to cover the doubt. How did she know I'd be here? I wondered why she had chosen that moment to surprise me – and why?

The lecturer broke off to make a fulsome introduction of me to his students, waving an arm at me as he spoke in rapid Spanish. The students all turned to look at me, and as he spoke I recognised only my name and Valdez's.

I glanced at Francine and she held my gaze, reading my reaction. I smiled. There was something else too with Francine, which as ever I couldn't quite determine. As the lecturer addressed final questions from the students and I looked ahead I sensed her folding her arms, studying me. I felt that her glance was part incredulous, part analytical. As the lecturer offered explanations, as if a mental avenue of her own choosing had become too arduous, Francine threw her long and slightly dry mane of long, dark hair over to the other side of her head. As I sensed her look to the stage I took a moment to study her.

Her red dress was functional, rather than fashionable, the white t-shirt under it in perfect fitting with the students. It somehow pained me to think that the students might think of the woman, whose accomplished mind surprised me on a daily basis, as one of their own.

On the way out she anticipated my approach with an intense expression. The mischief playing around her lips grew stronger.

'Well, this is a surprise,' I said.

She slouched against the stack. 'A good one, I hope?' she asked, rolling her eyes.

I remember the pinched quality to her voice, the slight mealy tone to it. As she looked for my reaction I remembered as well the blend of recrimination, exasperation and intensity that I often associated with her.

A couple of students lingered close to me. When one heavy-browed Greek woman asked in English about my current book I felt a sense of panic rise. As I tried to form an answer, Francine caught the question without batting an eyelid. Her smile towards the student was proficient and sudden. 'No decent novel can be explained with a pithy answer,' she said. 'You should take his answer as proof it's worth reading.'

Once they left, her hands went to her hips.

'So – is this business or pleasure?' I asked.

She offered me a lopsided smile. 'I know you're having an expenses-paid holiday, but that doesn't make you James Bond,' she said.

'Touché.'

'Though I would like to go over some proofs with you. Don't pretend *all this*,' she said, waving around her, 'takes up more than an hour of your day.'

'No, I don't,' I said.

'You have a month here – I thought you'd be glad of something to do.'

'In fact, there's been a development on that front.'

'What do you mean?'

'All I'm saying is, you were right to tell me to get my contract translated.'

She pretended to throw herself against the wall, and I laughed. 'Of course,' she whispered, tucking a spilt lock of hair over her ear.

'Shall we go out to dinner?' I said. 'I'll explain.'

I realise now, looking back at the scene, that I never did find out how she knew I'd be at that lecture.

5

We ate linguine on a restaurant overlooking the sea which, as expected, she had chosen long in advance. The wind from the ocean, visible beyond the drop behind her, seemed to only disturb the tips of her hair.

Between mouthfuls she held her knife and fork up in a way that unnerved me. I remembered how Francine's presence had a sense of intention about it that I hadn't seen before. It often seemed like she was suppressing something she might give in to at any moment – it was in the sudden change of expressions.

It occurred to me that in films characters walk into a story and it is only circumstances that really reveal them. Writers are too cowardly to show people as blades and so they let the world do the work of unsheathing people in their stories. But Francine wouldn't fit into a film. She is a real person – in the best and worst sense of the word. She can walk off the screen at any point, walk off the balcony into the sea, punch you, start crying, and any choice she made would be done with utter sincerity. You might not like what she was saying at a given moment, but with time I had found her acuity indisputable.

As we made our way through the dishes she talked about how she was redrafting her chapters, how she was assimilating new information into them, and which publishers were accepting submissions all in one torrent.

I have often thought that my best attribute is the fact Francine thought me worthy of her time. During mental binges of self-loathing I would see a message from her and think I must have redeeming features because she would not keep sifting through the dusty rubble of my mind if there was nothing in there. If she is sitting opposite you it is because she thinks there is something to glean from you.

But the force of her speech soothed me. I looked past her, at the rich blue of the early evening sky. As Francine recounted recent meetings I watched a golden haze rise from the crescent of the bay, its rim speckled with walking people. The light shade of the blue water was speckled with boats closer to the shore. Francine sipped the wine and her narrowed eyes suggested scrutiny of the taste. As ever, I wondered how many of her perceptions she kept hidden.

I remembered the first time we slept together. It was after a late-night writing session over a bottle of Rioja and a Chinese takeaway. Afterwards, the air sticky with prawn crackers, we'd been piling up those foil boxes and her elbow had touched mine.

She'd looked up at me, rapt and yet deeply critical, and I kissed her. Her response had been generous enough to be immediate – Francine was not a coward when it came to the body and the heart. When I tore off her shirt she nodded in approval and stripped off my belt. I thought of a circus tamer cracking a whip, and all the lions leaping in time to a single motion. I was surprised by my hunger for a body that long looked untameable. As we had sex I realised that I was only getting the narrow aspects of her temperament and sensuality that, in some deft calculus, she had deemed my due at this moment. Whenever we had sex afterwards – and it was only when she decided to kiss me – I felt as if I was with a different person. That was how labyrinthine she was.

The food and wine were invigorating in my stomach. As we finished the bottle I looked at Francine; the way the sunlight illuminated the hanging curtain of her dark hair. The impish freckles, the sudden surges of impatience as she articulated herself. Something was forming on her face, some sentiment she had at last deemed it time to share.

'So, what's this extra work they've got you doing?' she asked.

I thought of what happened after the first time we had sex. How she'd put her clothes back on with a calmness that revealed she had planned for it all. She had anticipated the audacity of flesh tearing into flesh, mouths roving over arms and thighs, tongues merging. She knew it brought a shared sense of outrage that never quite dissipates. Yet for all that there had been no acknowledgement of the strangeness of two friends, two collaborators, having now slept together. Somehow, she had contained it with the effortless peristalsis of a great anticipator. Francine had mapped the trajectory of our relationship and where our intimate moments lay on it long ago. I wondered what else she had in mind for me.

'Extra work?' I asked, playing for time.

This is what she had come here to ask.

I sighed, and explained. Anaesthetising myself from embarrassing moments in the story with heavy gulps of wine.

6

'So this vice-chancellor is clearly getting a cut of the finished collection,' she said. 'Why else would he care about setting up the award?'

'You think?' I asked, gripping my wine glass.

She toyed with the stem of her glass.

'Think about it,' she said, looking up at me. 'He's assigned to be the guardian of Valdez's literary estate, but he's not given any oversight of the book. He's either a very committed friend, or there's something in it for him. Why would he neglect to mention that *only you* can sign off the book?' She sipped. 'He was probably hoping that you'd just sign if off, given Maria wouldn't have mentioned that important detail.'

'But she *did* mention the detail.'

'Yes. On which note – she seems particularly committed to the legacy of a grandfather who, by her own admittance, she only recently got to know.'

'Which is why she's particularly committed. Know-it-all.'

'Hmm. It does beg the question of whether she got close to him when she realised someone was about to inherit a fortune. I'll bet she has a personal interest in this book too.'

'You're very suspicious of these people. Maybe she just wants to do right by him. Follow his dying wish?'

Francine leant back. 'Well, I don't know this Maria. But I know a bit about the vice-chancellor of this place.'

I take a pensive sip.

'Like what?'

She looked over at the ocean. 'You know, before I came to your lecture I attended a debate the students were in. Got talking to a few of them that confidently spoke English. You know what I noticed?'

'Go on.'

'They have *exactly* the same problems as the students back home have. High debt, courses under huge financial pressure to bring in overseas students. Students with a fierce, but often toothless voice. An older generation with all the housing who had all the best wages telling themselves that because the younger ones have i-phones both generations had it just as hard. I was struck in particular by one student doing a PhD with a supervisor who didn't have one himself, in fact who'd failed his many times. Who, I was told, used his position at the university as the head of a course to spend as much time as possible basking in the attention of young, attractive female students and aggrandising his own reputation, which was built on very slender academic credentials.'

'Sounds to me like some academics have a mindset that is very out of date. They want to feel like they're in ivory towers; untouchable, indulged.'

She cleared her throat, and I wondered if she had practised that speech. Something about the assurance in each lull and surge suggested she had.

She swilled the wine around in her glass. 'They are a dying breed but it's amazing the influence such charlatans are allowed to have. These students know they are about to go into a job market where they'll be competing with the rest of the world. They know they need far more skills and experience to get the job their parents had at their age and that even if they get it, they won't get the cheap housing and strong economy their parents enjoyed. They know that even if they get the job, it'll be low-wage, with no job security, and that the debt will never really lift. And they're often kissing the asses of dilettantes who in turn tell them they're brilliant to feel that they look good in their eyes. But men like that training them; they have very limited academic knowledge themselves. The students are being played.'

The way she looked at me suggested she had now got to the crux of her concern.

'You do remember how all that feels, don't you, Jude?'

I leant back.

'I don't think that tells us much about this Velasco. What you've described is the same across Europe.'

'Well,' she said, her voice almost too quiet to hear. 'These students made one thing very clear to me. That in the world of self-interested, overpaid vice-chancellors this Marco Velasco is in another league.'

'How?'

'20,000 Euros of expenses a year. One and a half million Euros a year in wages. A grace and favour flat. A second for his current mistress. A Bentley.'

'Yeah, so he's overpaid. What's new?'

'Yeah. A baby boomer who *in principle* wants to help the younger generation while having no idea they can't start to make the money he has. And while his students' debts skyrocket, and their grants are lower than ever. Two of his students even committed suicide, with news reports saying their debts were a big a factor.'

Christ, I thought. Is there anything she doesn't know?

'Yet somehow he can find 16,000 Euros for *you* to live here for a month,' she said.

'Hmm.'

She leant forwards, knitting her fingers together. 'You think he suddenly grew a sense of social responsibility when his friend died?' She shook her head. 'There's something going on.'

'Like what?'

'I don't know.' She looked out at the sea. 'Like he gave Valdez a load of money from the university if in return he got to be executor of his estate. But Valdez didn't like this arrangement, and left a sting in the tail when he realised he didn't want an asshole in control of his last collection. Hence —' she spread her arms at me. 'You.'

She put her hands behind her head. I remembered her doing that after sex, the glow in her expression.

'So when you tell me he's been using the university's money to get someone to finish a book by his best friend, it tells me two things, Jude. One – he *has* to do that. Two – there's something in it for him.'

I felt my brow crumple. 'I think you're letting your imagination run away with you, Francine,' I say, while realising that any hunches she has had in the past have turned out to be right.

'Maybe he honestly thought you were the only person who'd get what he was going for in this collection. Or maybe the collection is some complex puzzle that he thinks only you can crack. So have you had a look at it yet?'

'Tomorrow. Was meant to be today, but she put me off.'

Francine smiled. 'She's trying to make it look presentable. My hunch is – it'll be an indulgent mess.'

'You think?'

'Yeah. Everyone involved knows *you* can be blamed if the published version is a mess. I think the vice-chancellor is using you as a patsy. He knows he'll get his cut, whatever happens.'

I cracked my knuckle. 'Christ. You could be right. But what's to stop me just signing it off so I get a pay cheque?'

She took a breadstick from the jar, and bit off the end. 'The guilty conscience that I know you'd have. Not to mention the sense of shame because people would then blame you for doing a shoddy job with your favourite writer's final collection.'

My first thought being *so what*. But, as is so often the case with Francine, I know she is onto something.

'I hate that you know all this.'

'I might be wrong.'

'I need to read this bloody thing,' I say.

She raised an eyebrow. 'So what's this Maria like?'

I wondered how to word my response. In the end I decided she would get to the truth, regardless.

'She seems pretty mixed up by this whole situation.' I said. 'Tense. She didn't sound happy with the vice-chancellor either.'

'That figures. So – do you think you could work with her?'

Her gaze seemed to shake a little as it settled on me.

'Hopefully. She's a qualified academic, at least.'

Francine exhaled. 'I'm telling you. However academic she seems, there'll be more than loyalty that's motivating her.'

I wiped my brow. 'Yeah, like you said, I'm a patsy.'

Francine touched my elbow. 'You're the man your favourite writer trusted with his final work. You might have agreed to look over —'

'Overlook,' I corrected.

She nodded, 'Okay, overlook his final work. But your money here isn't dependent on you signing the book off.'

'I have a feeling the other 8000 Euros won't be forthcoming if I don't.'

She smiled.

'Then you'll need to do what your conscience tells you. I suggest you take a look at this book, first chance you get. And you need to find out if this Maria and Velasco are getting a cut. You might have to meet him.'

'Easily done. I'm going to be introduced to him at the awards ceremony.'

She nodded. 'I suspect he'll have more than a passing interest in how the book is getting on,' she said. 'Perhaps he makes no money from the estate except from this book. Remember – you don't *have* to give him anything. He's stuffing your mouth with other people's gold. It amazes me how adept some people in positions of power at the university in using the mechanics of their roles to indulge themselves. And there's so little left for that generation – *our generation* – that the temptation for us to fight each other over the scraps we do have becomes, I don't know.' She seemed to drift off for a moment, as if her mind were following the smoke of a distant fire, not one that was burning in her. 'Irresistible.'

She finished her wine. 'Send me that contract again – I'll get someone else to translate it. Just to be on the safe side.'

I nodded, and took the final breadstick.

'Are you okay?' she asked.

I looked out at the ocean. With a squint, it could have been the sea I'd lived next to as a child, on a hot day.

'Do you remember the first conversation we had?'

'About how you'd swim in the sea after school?'

'Yes, that one.'

Francine's smile suggested she had replayed the conversation in her mind as well.

'I remember telling you how I would get up in the middle of the night and walk through the village,' she said. 'How I would climb up onto the roof of my house and stay there. Thinking my morbid thoughts all night. I remember then realising that I hadn't shared that with anyone before.'

I cradled my wine glass.

'Why do you think we did stuff like that?'

'Christ, I don't know.'

'Come on. Humour me.'

She leant back in her chair. 'Why did we skive off school, stay up all night, go walking through the dark? Sit on beaches in the dark waiting for the day to start?'

'Yeah – why did we?'

She touched my hand. 'Sounds to me like two people who weren't getting enough from the situation they were in,' she said.

7

I sat on the balcony, sipping a beer from the two bottles I'd placed in a bucket at the foot of the sun lounger. I watched the sun fade behind the tall buildings of the city, hefts of brick and glass that held the warmth of the day. Francine had gone to meet an old friend, leaving me alone with my thoughts.

I was wondering what my next step should be when the bell rang.

Kimberly was standing on the doorstep, with a pensive expression. Her shining gold hair and pink, glossy lips were immaculately arranged. The fitted black trousers, cutaway black top and matching stilettos all made me suspect she had just left a shoot.

'Sorry to bother you,' she said. 'But I've got a tiny emergency.'

'Are you okay?'

'My phone has died and they haven't switched on my Wi-Fi yet.' Her features arranged into a subtle look of pleading. 'Is there any chance I could use your laptop – just to send one email?'

As she tapped at the laptop on the kitchen table I resumed sipping my beer. A couple of minutes later she came out to join me, anticipating the sun by putting on a pair of black vintage sunglasses. 'You saved my life,' she said, moving closer.

'Come on, it's no problem. So what happened?'

She folded her hands as she looked at the skyline. Her nails were pristine – painted in a firm shade of pink.

She looked at the beer.

'Would you like one?' I asked, motioning at the lounger next to mine.

There was a split second where her face crumpled, before she composed herself.

'I would love one,' she whispered.

I pulled the top off the spare beer and handed it to her. Sunlight caught the gold liquid inside as she took a deep draught. She smiled, as if satisfied, before she sat on the other lounger. She placed her long legs out in front of her. I tried not to stare at them, but was bewitched by their length and strength. Her physique seemed somehow more than human.

She unbuckled her heels and slipped them off her feet with a sigh.

'I had a bit of a panic,' she said, staring out. 'I started the shoot today, even though the company still haven't paid me.'

'That's terrible,' I said, wondering what on earth Francine would make of the spectacle when she returned. Something told me not to allow Kimberley to look too comfortable.

'Yeah,' she said, her voice taking on a slight American lilt. 'I'd checked my bank balance and was at my limit. I needed to chase them up and without my phone working I had no way to do it.'

'It's all sorted now, though?'

She nodded. I noticed some pale freckles on her nose, obscured by her rich, deep tan.

'My agent swears all the money will be paid at midnight.' She crossed her legs. 'The thing is – I've got debts to pay and I can't hold off any longer. So she'd better be right.'

'I can't believe such a huge company would be reluctant to pay.'

She nodded. 'They're actually the worst. It's unbelievable. They've been promising this money for months. And the whole time my agent's been on maternity. She's a right ballbreaker, so I reckon if she'd been at work they'd have paid. But by *not* paying they forced me to shell out for *everything*. I had to pay for gym access every day—' she says, motioning over her body, 'to keep in shape as there's a stringent examination I have to go through on that. I've had to pay for the flight here, pay for the flat. And after all that there's no Internet, no hot water.

Nothing. I had to get ready on the shoot. Turned up looking like a right scram.'

'You're welcome to use the facilities here, if you want to.'

I regretted the offer when I remembered Francine. Kimberley picked up on my look with a sceptical glance, compounding the awkwardness.

I decided to go on another tack.

'So they're going to pay you again at the end of the shoot, yeah?'

For the first time she really smiled. It looked like a load had been lifted from her shoulders. 'I'm getting it all in one go.'

I sipped the beer. 'You look like someone with a plan.'

'I am,' she said. Through the glasses, I saw her squint at the skyline. 'The thing is – I'm giving up modelling. Getting back to my studies. That's what most of this money is for – to pay off my debts, then to pay my tuition for my first year.'

'So this is your modelling swansong?'

She nodded. 'Yep. And wouldn't you just know it? It's everything I ever hated about modelling. Bullshit promises, loads of physical pain, and at the end of it relief instead of any sense of satisfaction.'

'I can't believe how much these corporations are allowed to shaft people these days.'

She looked at me. 'But from what I hear you don't need to worry about that anymore? Your friend was saying something about a big award you've won.'

'Well, I've only got half of the money. 8000 Euros. Finally paid off some of my debts too.'

'Funny, isn't it,' she said, tilting her head towards me. 'At my age my parents didn't need to get into any debt to keep their heads above water. They saved for three years to buy their house. My flat has developed damp in the time I've been living in it and its rent has gone up. I'm already in a flat share with three, on the same street there was a billboard I was in.'

'That's surreal.'

'If my rent goes up any more I wonder if I'll be on the street.'

'I feel for you. I can't remember not worrying about money – I thought about getting a trade but everyone I know with one was unable to leave their parents' home given the wage stagnation. I don't get the rest of the money unless I sign off this book some author left behind.'

My dismissal of Valdez, to try and look impressive in front of a model, felt unfaithful.

The sunlight caught her blonde hair for a second, before the glare eased behind a building. She looked around her. 'It looks to me like you're doing alright.'

'Well, there's harder ways to make money, I suppose,' I said.

'Yeah, like commercial modelling.' She closed her eyes.

'Right,' I answered.

8

'Come in,' Maria said, stepping behind her oak door.

I caught a glimpse of a low-beamed room, its centre filled with a semicircle of soft couches. Getting to the top floor of the house had made me out of breath, but I tried to hide it. I caught a glimpse of the sea between the houses in the far window.

I realised Maria's apartment was deceptively large. The desk on the left, piled with books, filled just one annex of the living room. I wondered if the volumes were all her grandfather's.

She picked up a sheaf of papers from the desk. Her hair was pinned up in an elaborate lattice, and the strappy white top revealed tanned shoulders. A brown, glossy pencil skirt seemed a little too stylish for studying. 'Here it is,' she said.

I took the papers from her. This collection has to be 150 pages, at most, I thought. How hard could it be to sign off?

I looked at the coversheet. On the front page was the single word – 'Lacuna.'

'So in what sense is this collection a lacuna?'

She sat in the chair at the desk, and rifled through a packet of cigarettes.

'I suppose it signifies the unfilled gap of his career. Of everything he wanted to do as a writer.' She lit up, and inhaled. 'He's acknowledging the gap between what he wanted to say and how far he got in saying it. He left it to the rest of us to bridge that gap.'

As she looked over at it I realised her expression was very different from the one she had had when we'd first met. Heavier. Her eyes had faint dark rings under them. As she inhaled again it occurred to me that her beauty had, until recently, not been contingent. A result of good genes; talent merging with beauty. But the Faustian pact within that mingling led to poisoned legacies like this one. Judging from the filled ashtray on the desk, it was clearly testing her.

Had she spent the night reading over the book? If so how could it have affected her so much?

I flickered through the pages. Even at a glance, it was the strangest collection I had ever seen. Some of the stories were short – just a few lines long. They lacked syntax. The words were like fragments scattered on the page. Is this even prose, I wondered?

Other stories were actually arranged on the page in fragments, or with sloping line endings, that rose and fell like waves.

'Surely stories like this have to be complete, to have such a shape?' I asked, holding the sheaf up.

She turned her head into the smoke. 'Try following them,' she said. 'He wasn't being easy on the reader – or the editor. The presentation of stories like that suggest they are complete but their content demands the *reader* finish them.'

'Not the first time he's done that. In *Interiors* he almost leaves the reader to choose the ending.'

'Yes, but the preface explains what choices they should make in that book.' She removed a hair from her lip. 'He wasn't so generous here.'

There was a faint scent of perfume on the book, and I realised that blossoms from the ivy brushing against the open window were mixing with that scent. As Maria drew closer to me the scent of her perfume grew stronger. I tried to concentrate. I flickered through the rest of the pages. Some dense chunks of text mingled with pages that looked more and more fragmented as it went on.

'I feel like I've entered a labyrinth.'

'Oh,' she said, drawing on the cigarette. 'You have. This is the entry point.'

'To what?'

She smiled sweetly. 'To his mind.'

I tried to judge the ambiguity with which she had made the remark. There was a note of admiration, with a harmonised note of exhaustion. It was only later that I understood that if there was any exhaustion, then it would come from me. From a sense of cleansing needed after immersing yourself too deeply in the minutiae of another human being, a sense of being misted in their essence. Surely all artists strive to achieve this sense of intimacy with their reader, on their own verbose and selfish terms?

'So can I take it home?'

'As long as you look after it. His will prohibited anyone making any copies.'

'No problem.'

'I need some fresh air, actually,' she said, stubbing out the cigarette in an empty mug. 'I'll walk you to the bus stop.'

9

'So has Marco read this yet?'

I wondered why she was looking around herself as we walked. The streets were almost empty. Why would it matter if anyone heard us?

'The will specified only you and I can read it. And that you *only* read it during the month you're here. You know that if any of the terms are broken then responsibility for the book defaults to Velasco. And that's a situation I think he'd be only too happy with.'

'Why do you think your grandfather was so specific in his will?' I asked, refusing a flier from a man outside a diner.

She didn't answer.

'I don't get why he wouldn't want his best friend to read it, but would demand that a total stranger pass judgement on it.'

'My grandfather's relationship with Marco was a bit complicated. I don't have all the answers. But I know Marco dearly wants us to finish this book this month.'

'So he can get paid once it's published?'

Her expression was sad and pure, like a commercial from your childhood.

'Yes,' she said. 'Money is what drives him. Money and power.'

She glowered for a moment, and then looked at me with a blend of hurt and concern. 'I suppose without him you wouldn't be here.' Her hands clasped together, as we passed vendors closing their kiosks. There was a roar of shutters coming down. 'And we wouldn't be working with each other,' she added.

I wondered if something was being added in translation. What was she implying?

'I must admit; I don't like what I've heard about this Marco so far.' She gave nothing away. 'You have to admit', I pressed, 'People like him just look after their own interests…'

Maria looked at her feet.

'People like that created the world we live in,' she said. 'Look around you.'

She stopped and looked at me. The vibrant green in her eyes, even in the dusk, intoxicated me. She smiled, and touched my arm. 'You're not going to ruin this for us, are you?'

'Us?'

I wondered if she was unaware of the romantic implications of the word, in English.

She smiled. The drawn aspect of her face seemed to have vanished. 'I know it's not going to be easy, and the book will be hard to make sense of. But you have a month, and it's only a hundred or so pages.'

'150.'

She skipped ahead, before whirling towards me. 'Besides, isn't there part of you that finds it exciting to be part of some great plan? Some big, secretive operation? My grandfather was a genius, and you and I are a part of it.' She spread her arms. 'So many people in this world will read – not just read but *devour* – something that you and I will have completed. You don't need to understand every aspect of it to appreciate we're part of something amazing. The final collection of a truly great writer. Even if his work has the solipsism of a narcissist about it – and even if I struggle to get past that, think of it as an empathic work of art, I think my grandfather left us a wonderful gift.'

'Perhaps because of the role he casts us in? In making us characters?'

She stopped, and looked at me. I detected various components in her expression – excitement – tiredness. Fear. 'It's like the start of an adventure, isn't it?' she said, pleading.

'An adventure?'

'Yes. Or at least an exploration. You have to bear in mind; I can't get to know him any more now. My only chance to know him while he was alive was brief. But how many grieving people get to carry on the dialogue with someone once they're gone? I'm getting that chance. By trying to complete this whole thing – it's like a bonding exercise.'

I nodded, and felt dizzy. Her statement seemed one of a person immersed in grief. Someone using her emotions to try to will a dead man back into life, with this book offering her the means to do that. While understandable, this act of desperation felt somehow indecent. Given that he had checked out of the dialogue, this felt like a forced conversation which, to continue, required her to ventriloquise on his behalf.

'Okay. That's exactly how I'm going to look at it,' I said. 'An adventure. One that I am lucky to be on.'

My tone was more sarcastic than I'd intended, but she looked relieved. I knew that behind her grief were other pressures, adding to the miasma that I could not see over her shoulder, but knew was there. Maria leant forward, and kissed me on the cheek.

'Relieved to hear you say that,' she said.

For a moment, as her body leant against mine, I distinctly felt that she was shaking.

10

I hadn't moved off the black leather couch for four and a half hours, for trying to make sense of the manuscript. Whenever I finished a few pages I placed them on the glass table next to me – and Francine got up from the kitchen table to get them.

Her body language betrayed nothing as she returned to her chair to absorb them. My concerns around breaking the terms of Valdez's will by sharing the book with her dissipated once she had seen it resting on the table. I knew that the moment she offered to read the collection I would not deny her for long. I felt so far out of my depth that involving her seemed the only chance I had of making sense of this situation.

The last few pages were a real slog. Valdez had a tendency to create in the reader a need for something to happen in the story, only for the opposite to then take place. He had, for some reason, decided I was the only person that could solve this puzzle of what should be left in – why was I his ultimate reader? Was it something I had – or didn't have? But all I wanted to do was rewrite passages to give them opposite conclusions. Characters he seemed to have created for us to root for were left disappointed, damaged without salvation. Characters we resented were given everything they desired and more. I went through believing this was perversity, having sensed too much empathy in the prose to conclude that. It reminded me, somehow, of a line from The Bible; a text which I felt guilty for not being more familiar with. 'For him who has will more be given, and he will have abundance; but for him who has not, even what he has will be taken away.' Was Valdez here forcing a kind of spiritual development onto us, by forcing us to accept a greater design at play, when we saw those he had made us loathe prosper? Or was he merely leaving something incomplete, so we willed ourselves to put the final piece in place, thereby merging with the text? Was he therefore achieving a kind of inextricable intimacy with us, without us realising?

My final fragile hypothesis about his mindset when writing it had been that it was just a showcase for all his writing ability, but its brevity put paid to that.

The collection felt like one long exercise in engendering desire only to make the reader question it.

I got to the final page, and as I scanned over it realised I was convincing myself that a vague understanding of it all was sufficient. I was almost unable to make sense of its final lines:

The opening to this story was written not knowing how it would end. But now it is completed (and it is) it is clear that the opening was only a premise. Why did you decide to interpret it as though it was not? Your interpretation was false. I decided the story would end here because it was always that way.

I placed the final page on the kitchen table, for Francine, and went back to my seat. I just didn't understand. He had removed any possibility that the piece had been left unfinished, by affirming it was completed. So why had he appointed me? Furthermore, how could he know what premise the reader had at the start of it? How could he be sure it was false? If he had crafted the story to offer a premise, why would he confirm that to be the case?

Francine snapped the last page down on the table.

'Some of his best writing is in this one. But my only conclusion,' she said, 'is that he doesn't want this collection to be finished by anyone. Even you. And if you're thinking about the whole Roland Barthes 'the greatest text is completed by the reader' thing then how come only *you* are the reader? The most he could've known about you – and I don't mean to be rude – is that you wrote some minor works about him. By appointing you to finish it he is saying you are the person who could get closest to completing this collection.'

I wanted to scream, but resisted. Why was she always two steps ahead of me?

I glanced out at the city, cooling after the onslaught of the day's heat. It soothed my eyes to fix on a distant skyline. It was only at the end of the document that I had realised how much my eyes were aching.

As Francine turned in her bar stool towards me, her hands dropped between her thighs. 'So – what do you think?'

'He carefully creates a desire in the reader, a need for a certain conclusion, only to frustrate it. He's making the point that a book is never finished, that characters live on in the reader.'

She raised an eyebrow. 'And do these characters have bills to pay?'

'Okay. I think he is saying that works of the imagination can't be resolved. By creating the ultimate conundrum – and ensuring it can't be finished – particularly not in a month – he's ensuring there is no 'last word' from him. So that as a writer, he remains a live proposition. Even in death. It's an ultimate work of ego, of legacy building.'

'But then isn't that just an indictment on artistic will generally?'

Another thought occurred to me; one I felt for some reason reluctant to share. Was it possible that he knew how I had felt in my early career? That he had guessed the feelings I would be unable to express even when validated? Had he taken me to this point of validation because he had known that I, and I alone, would understand how a writer's work is never completed? The message I was starting to get was that a body of work never says all an artist wants to express. That it is a mistake to assume that.

Was that the point he wanted to make?

I stood up, and moved to the window.

'There is something about this that only *you* can solve. Otherwise, he wouldn't have appointed you,' Francine said.

'Unless the point is that even I can't solve it?'

'In which case – you try for a month, tell Maria it can't be done, and you lose the 8000 Euros. Big deal. You still had this experience.'

I turned and looked at her. I had never been in a situation before where Francine wasn't sure of the solution. It scared me. When reading Valdez I had always been overawed. His writing had always taken me into new realms. They were confusing to be in at first but in the end I gained clarity over these places. I felt like a better person for having had an experience that had altered me. Would this collection offer people that feeling? Or was it possible that even after the month ended, this work would torture me for life? The collection was certainly unnerving Maria.

I leant against the glass. Perhaps this award would make me famous without me achieving anything. Thereby exposing the fallacy of fame. Did he *want* me to lose my mind?

I winced, and closed my eyes. Perhaps that was the price of fame; the sense that you never deserve it.

'You know I'm right,' Francine whispered.

'Yeah, and I hate that.'

She shook her head.

'So this vice-chancellor doesn't get his money, and Maria doesn't get whatever she wants. How's that your problem?'

I thought of Maria's face. The relief on it when I had told her I would take on the challenge. Had the book already got to her? Was she keen to transfer it to me before it drove her mad? Perhaps to her it was just about money. I decided I would ask her.

'Forget it for the rest of the night,' Francine said. 'Let the story sit with you. Enjoy being in a beautiful flat in Barcelona. Who says you have to crack it all in one go?'

I nodded, and cut past her for the fridge. 'Did I mention that the woman living opposite me happens to be here modelling for some huge mobile phone ad?'

'Lucky you.'

'That's not what I'm saying.'

I opened a beer, and moved back to the couch.

Francine moved over to me, exaggerating her trailing movements. The light, white summer dress with its faint, thin stripes threatened to fall from her body. I sat back in the couch. As she sat on my lap, I smoothed her hair, which emanated from a loose plait. As her thighs clenched on my lap I was surprised by her subtle physical power – I'd forgotten it. She tweaked my nose and I wondered if up close her face was garish. It was only in the intensity of one of her smiles that it seemed that way. Otherwise the pliant lips and the glacial green eyes were seductive.

'Glad to hear it,' she said.

'Anyway – as models go this one is particularly disgruntled. She's been utterly shafted by the company she's working for.'

Poking me in the chest, she said, 'Too many people are driven by money.' She nuzzled her nose on my cheek. 'You get your award tomorrow,' she said. 'You should ask Velasco what he's really getting out of all this.'

'Hmm.'

She flopped down on the couch at my side, and buried her face in a pillow.

'You have to tell Velasco what you think of him face-to-face,' she said.

'You could do it? I have a plus one,' I said.

'I never turn down a free dinner,' she said, flipping over. She looked over at me, her dark hair a thin veil over her face. 'Although are you sure you don't want to take this model instead?' she asked.

'It's not like that. Her flat has no hot water. Or Internet. She cleaned herself up, we chatted and she went home.' I sat up straight. 'What's the big deal?'

'The big deal is – you don't realise when you are being played. Ever. She's playing you. She's probably lonely. But you're not. Because I'm here.'

'Yes, you are. Lucky me.'

She grimaced, and threw a pillow at me. I tried to tear it from her hands, and she smiled as we struggled. Her moans sounded sexual, and as I nuzzled into her neck she clasped my head into it with a soft cry. As I kissed her, her exposed legs kicked up out of the sofa and wrapped around my back. 'I like it when we argue,' she said, drawing breath. 'It reminds me we're not just another stuffy, bourgeoisie couple.'

Afterwards, Francine trailed into the bathroom. She seemed unbothered by her nudity in front of the vast windows. Her thighs had a hint of muscularity to them that was a little shocking, and it made the twist of hair at the top of her back look a little silly. I couldn't believe I had just had such intimacy with such a powerful force. When she came out, any traces of makeup on her face had been washed off. Her freckles shone as she approached me, the towel wrapped around her breasts. I realised I had been standing at the window, struggling to finish my warm beer.

'You okay?' she asked, drying her hair with the tips of the towel. I wondered how I would have felt without her. Completely lost, I decided.

'It's just–' I said. 'I'm really glad you're here.'

She looked baffled. 'What do you mean?'

I leant against the window. 'I thought this whole trip was going to be one big victory march. But I actually feel like I've been placed in some huge maze. And without you in it – I'd be lost!'

'And don't you forget it,' she said, turning towards the kitchen. She stops. 'On that note – can I ask you something?'

'Of course.'

She fetched a bottle of water from the fridge. 'You're worried about letting down this Maria, aren't you? You don't owe her anything, you know.'

I nod. 'I know that. But she's the granddaughter of my favourite writer. The man who inspired me in the first place. So if I can possibly–'

'Yeah, and she makes a fortune if she gets you to sign this thing off,' Francine interrupted, pointing a finger at me. 'Don't forget that it's probably money that is making her tick.'

'You don't know her.'

I thought of the way our bodies had mingled. The fluids that had mixed, the kisses that seemed unfinished, left on one another.

Something flashed across her eyes. 'Are you saying you do?'

'No! Not at all.'

'Because you do know she could be trying every trick in the book to get you to do what she wants.' She placed her hands on her hips. 'And I do mean *every* trick.'

I walked over, and kissed her on the head. She smelt of expensive soap. She didn't respond to the gesture. I held her head in my hands. 'I get it,' I said.

As I leant back I asked myself what was happening in my relationship with her. That gesture had felt wrong, a defilement of the equality we had long maintained. Since when did I reassure her? She always reassured me – with impatience and even aggression. Vulnerability only came from her in barbed remarks – never in remarks that were unadorned. When had the relationship changed from two colleagues occasionally having sex to … whatever this was?

She pulled away from me, and walked towards the balcony.

I remember what it felt like sitting out there before she arrived.

'You'll meet her at the ceremony tomorrow,' I said. 'And you'll see what I mean.'

11

'This isn't right,' Francine said, looking around the dining hall. She gestured around the long dining table that we, and a crowd of visiting guests, had just sat at. I wanted her to lower her voice.

'Gold plates, seven course meals, while female students turn to stripping to pay tuition fees,' she hissed. She pointed out a bulky man in his late forties, taking off a grubby looking beanie hat and wiping his bald head before replacing it. His heft dwarfed a small, blonde student of his who, with a supercilious smirk, he seemed to be teasing with the idea that he was bemused by what she was saying. 'That's the lecturer I was told about,' she said. 'Failed his PhD three times, but somehow decides who else gets to have PhDs. Only ever seen giving the time of day to young, female students of his. When they want his time he has hours of attention to give them, but if anyone else wants his help, he's far too busy. Then constantly claims his female students are in love with him.'

'Hasn't an academic got a thriving literary career of their own to tend to?'

'Well, he *makes out* he has. But scratch the surface and it's all self-published work in obscure publishing houses. But the empire-building of people like that in academia exists mainly in their mind, outside of which they're largely disregarded. I've mainly seen it in England. They can carry on like they're a huge deal and their younger, more unworldly students may even believe them because why would they know better?'

'I suppose they wouldn't.'

Her eyes narrowed; she'd stewed on this for a while, been passed over in favour of the bullishness of such men's apparent self-belief. 'I think some of these types get addicted to attention from the uncritical. And meanwhile they keep being their own gatekeeper.' She focused her eyes me, with an intensity that made me hope she never sent a critical blast of attention my way. 'It's a rot in academia,' she said. 'These academic settings that allow people to perpetuate their own mythology based on pretty much nothing beyond their need for self-gratification.'

As if he had sensed the glare of Francine's attention the man smiled and smirked knowingly at her. It felt like a gesture that he had convinced himself he imbued with enough charm to disarm any threat to his vision of himself. Francine looked away, her residual expression expressing disdain at the presumptive nature of his glare. She didn't see, but his gaze lingered down her body, considered her hips, back and buttocks. The sneer on his mouth seemed to react and say, 'she's not that attractive anyway,' and in turn dismiss any criticism from someone as perceptive as her. But I had the distinct suspicion there was more to it, as well. That the more robustly she rebuffed a man like him, the more he would tell people that she was in fact deeply attracted to him. The false claim made as the most narcissistic way of muting a potential critic as well as trying to increase his standing. But something told me not to share with her my unfounded theory and rankle her further with my half-baked theory.

She tucked a long tuft of hair over one ear, satisfied by the catharsis of her outburst. I felt uncomfortable in my suit, with the huge set of sharp keys and the wallet full of shrapnel bulging in one pocket. My mobile phone also felt heavy in the other pocket and I imagined myself looking as wide-hipped as a clown. I tried to adjust the three of them with my hand, causing Francine to blanche.

'Give them to me,' she said, 'You can't go up on stage like that.'

Twitching, I fished them out for her. In an oversized red jumper and black pedal pushers Francine had taken a very different approach to the dress code than Maria had.

At the far end of the hall I could see Maria in a skin-tight lace white dress, cut off at the arms. She was ensconced in a deep conversation with Velasco. I had not been surprised to see that he had matched the portrayal my imagination had conjured for him.

He was a swarthy, deep-tanned man; his belly poked out from a satin-lined gown. A thin semicircle of white hair lined the back of his head, making him appear a touch Roman. He had one hand on Maria's shoulder, but it seemed to me a bit close to her neck. Given her exposed shoulders, teased by the ringlets falling from pinned hair, the gesture looked intimidating. To complete the picture she looked terrified.

It struck me how, despite the room full of mingling people, her glance connected with mine from over twenty yards.

Francine folded her arms. 'And as for him. I hear he eats so much pâté that he has gout.'

'Ah yes,' I said, 'Comrade Velasco. Always acting on behalf of the people.'

'And in a few minutes you'll be shaking his hand and accepting an award off him. *Thanking* him,' she said.

Maria was pointing us out to Velasco. I noticed his lack of compulsion to follow her finger. His eyes were shamelessly fixed on her breasts.

'So, we know he has little *theoretical* interest in you then,' Francine whispered, as Maria made her way over.

Maria smiled, looking between the two of us as she stopped.

'Francine, this is Maria Valdez,' I said. 'Maria – this is Francine, my co-writer.'

'Co-writer?' Maria raised an eyebrow, Mediterranean in its size, scoring her wide eyes. 'You mean you two write together?' she said, as if this was the height of intimacy.

She looked between the two of us, her expression darkening.

'Francine and I are writing a philosophy book together. It's due at the publishers in a couple of months – so she's staying for a few days.'

'Well–' Francine said. 'I may stay longer than a couple of days.' She smiled up at Maria, hard. 'We'll see what happens.'

Maria nodded. 'You never mentioned you already had a co-writer, Jude,' she said, placing her hand on the table. Her nails were blood red, immaculate. She looked behind her, checking that Velasco hadn't heard our exchange.

'I hope you don't mind leaving him to me for just this one book, Francine?' she said, her voice dropping to a stage whisper. 'I'm sure he told you about all my grandfather's rules.'

Francine looked blank.

'How only him and I can see the collection?' Maria shielded her mouth behind her hand before she continued. 'The vice-chancellor was trying just now to convince me to show the book to him. But I don't want to give him anything to strengthen his hand.'

Francine nodded. 'Yes, we wouldn't want it getting out that those rules had been broken, would we?' she asked, looking at me.

Maria looked at me, with wide eyes. 'Well, *no*. Velasco would then have the power to put the book back in the vault, as the executor of the estate.' She looked at me with naked alarm. I was sure she was about to say my name.

'Don't worry,' Francine said, placing a hand on her arm. 'He wouldn't break the rules. We understand what this means to you.'

Flushing red, Maria choked the words 'thank you.' She rallied herself again – reminding me of some exotic plant that had just been splashed with water. 'This book probably means too much to me. To tell you the truth it has been … working me into the ground.'

'Well, you can hand it over to me now,' I said.

She exhaled. 'Thank you,' she said. 'So. Are you ready to meet the chancellor?'

Francine propelled me at the small of my back. 'Oh yes. More than ready,' she said.

I wondered if it was best to suggest going over alone. But the thought of leaving Maria with Francine was one that for some reason unsettled me. When did I hand over so much power to Francine, I wondered?

As the three of us approached, Velasco pushed a full canapé into his mouth. He suspended it there. Like a seal holding a fish in its jaw. 'Professor Velasco, please meet Jude Green,' Maria said.

12

I stood next to him, flanked by twitching accomplices, while a gulping man with the fragility of a vicar continued to gas on at him. Both ignored Maria's introduction. At one point Velasco glanced up and down Maria's legs, but his disinterested gaze didn't fall to Francine or me.

As I looked at him I considered what must have happened in his life to imbue him with such a sense of ease. In unguarded moments Francine, Maria and I would hunch, or tense. But his shoulders were thrown back, his head tilted back. He personified a state of confidence. I imagined the number of opportunities Velasco must have hoped for which had then come to pass for him to impart the sense that he would have whatever he wanted and there was no threat to him.

A glance at my watch confirmed that four shifting, unsettling minutes had passed before the vicar – his body language having long suggested impending departure – finally left Velasco's side.

'Professor Velasco – can I introduce Jude Green?' Maria asked, again.

He turned, his mouth half-open.

'The English writer,' he croaked, his eyes flitting over me.

'Good to meet you,' I said, holding out my hand. 'I am so grateful for the award.'

Francine's hand flashed to her mouth, as I realised I was shaking the tips of his fingers.

'*English*. You don't speak Spanish?'

I shook my head. He looked at Maria, irritable.

'So you are working very hard?' he grunted, looking me up and down with a raking stare.

His Spanish accent was so broad it was almost a cliché.

'I read the manuscript today,' I said.

He looked over my shoulder. 'Only today?'

I nodded.

'For a man of your education it should take a week at most,' he said, with an airy wave of his hand. He leant in, and put a palm on my shoulder. 'We have been very generous in the time we have afforded you.'

'You have; but it's a complex collection.'

He looked between Francine and Maria. 'How complex can a short story collection be, when it was written by a man in his second language!' he boomed, looking between Maria and Francine. 'It'll be his bestselling work. How would you put this? His *magnum opus*. And to have your second opinion – what harm can it do?'

I nodded. It was hard enough to engage with him, let alone ask what his stake in the book was. Sensing an impasse, Francine stepped forward.

'Francine Campbell – Jude's co-writer,' she said. 'As a fan of Valdez, I am so interested to know – had you been working together for long before he died?'

'As lifelong friends, yes,' he said, reaching for a wine glass.

Maria looked at Francine, her face paling.

'Did you read his work before he published it in the past?' she continued.

Valdez looked at Maria. He looked back at Francine.

'You have the physique of a dancer,' he said. 'Have you ever been told that before?'

'Never in an academic setting, no,' she said.

He glugged the wine. A drop of red snaked from the corner of his mouth and down his chin. He let it snake.

'I am also intrigued to know,' I began, cutting in, 'did you read all of Valdez's previous work? You two must've been very close for him to appoint you as executor.'

He looked at Maria. 'Executor? What is executor?'

In whispered Spanish, Maria explained.

He nodded. 'We were like *brothers*,' he said. He put his hand back on my shoulder. 'You know the thing about brothers? They share everything.'

'Like royalties?' Francine asked.

He looked her up and down. Maria closed her eyes.

'I have to make a speech,' Velasco said. He looked at me. 'A speech for *you*.'

Maria led him to the stage. As he walked onto it, behind her, I realised how short Velasco was. I thought of my own lacerating self-criticism, and yet how completely unabashed he seemed at his own waddle.

I could see no evidence of nerves as his hands spread around the lectern. Maria tilted the microphone over to him and he seemed to expect it. Her voice filled the room as she greeted us. The guests stopped chatting, and turned to her as she spoke in fluid Spanish. At one point she looked to her side, at Velasco.

The lecturer she had mentioned loomed behind Francine. He wore the same continual smirk, as if considering a narrative entirely separate to that which was in reality unfolding around him. I couldn't catch his name as he breathed something into Francine's hair. She winced and I feared what he'd said.

Francine focused on the stage.

The speech, also in Spanish, was brief and gruff. I recognised the mention of my name twice, and little else. At the last mention of my name, he pulled a gleaming trophy from behind the lectern, and his words of introduction caused laughter to ripple through the audience. Whatever brief mention of me had been made had clearly not been intended to be flattering.

'I got that last bit,' Francine whispered, leaning away from him and into me. 'He is saying he is sure the English would never let us down.'

The laughter turned to applause as he said my name again. An usher beckoned me onto the stage. As they did, I saw the smirking lecturer lean into Francine's hair and whisper something else. There was a thick, lingering scent coming off him, its source notes hard to define. I didn't want to leave her side, but he ignored my stare, his smile broadening. Francine looked at me with a sudden focus of the eyes that said 'Go,' the subtext being, 'don't patronise me, I can take care of myself.' At that, she swatted the hair the lecturer had been breathing into as if there was a fly.

At this he looked down, and shuffled his feet, adjusting his beanie hat over the back of his head. There was something laughable about the way this hulking man, dressed as if he was a teenager, looked at the stage while at the same time he was clearly determined to not offer an inch of his attention to another man for fear it might be at his expense. There was a mercurial fear in his eyes, the smarminess ready to flit into hostility.

Once I got close to Velasco I felt his hand on the small of my back. 'Look,' he whispered, waving out to the audience. 'They are rooting for you.'

I looked out and had to admit he was right. There was a sea of smiling faces in eveningwear, raising their hands as they applauded me. Velasco said my name one more time and the applause intensified. I got the clue he'd set me up as both a stooge and a joke.

As he shook my hand he smiled for cameras in the front row. 'Just smile,' he croaked. As I followed his command I saw Francine, a few rows back, folding her arms. Now Velasco would not let go of my hand.

He said my name again, loud, with a vigour that sounded almost sarcastic.

The crowd laughed and clapped. I felt the heat in my cheeks and I looked over at Maria, who was moving towards me with a smile. As photographers shouted their approval, she darted onstage and stood next to me. As the light bulbs flashed she put her arm around my shoulder. I stood there, rooted to the spot, as flash after flash captured my awkward position.

Francine, shaking her head, turned and walked out of the room.

13

My attempts to find her were thwarted by constant questions from journalists, asked in broken English. Why had Valdez chosen me? What was his last word book about? My urgent snatched scans across the room didn't locate her, and I started to panic. Did she realise she had my phone?

Maria appeared at my side, holding two flutes of champagne. 'Jude – there is someone you have to meet. Luis is a translator, and he was just telling me that he is planning to translate the book into Spanish.'

Don't we get a say, I wondered? I already knew, from the lurch in the pit of my stomach, who the man would be.

Behind her, the lecturer was swirling his wine as he looked into it.

'Good to meet you,' I said.

'Luis has translated the works of some famous poets. He did a new translation of Dostoevsky recently.'

'Luisa,' the man said, exaggerating the Spanish twang at the end of his name. 'And yes, I must concede she is correct; I did indeed collaborate with Dostoevsky.'

I winched – was this how self-aggrandisement was allowed to build – people were too polite to keep it in check?

Something in me loosened. 'Is it really a collaboration if he didn't agree to it?' I said.

'And though Spanish is my mother tongue,' he added, his gaze collecting Maria's features like a botanist looking at a rare plant as he looked past me, 'if I ever win a Pulitzer Prize I will collect it in Russian, given that my homeland refused to publish my work for so long, forcing me to go into exile.'

I longed for the proximity of Francine, to put this pretension on blast.

'Exile?' I said, struggling to get my head around this grandiosity. 'Like Nabokov?'

He handed his drink to a waitress who had been attending to someone else. 'Exactly like Nabokov. My home country forced me to undertake a literary rebirth by rejecting my thesis. I rose from the ashes like a Phoenix and had to play my trade,' he said, his fingers making inverted commas as he smirked down on me, 'with translation. Valdez's name carries a lot of weight. It is a name that I think *you* could really use.'

He inserted himself between me and Maria. 'And so tell me about yourself,' he said to her, turning his back on me.

Maria caught me shaking my head from over his shoulder. Excusing herself, she pulled me away.

Moments later we were sat on the stone steps of the hall, with Maria wrapping a fur stole around her shoulders. A thick lock of hair fell over her right eye as she turned to me.

'How are you feeling?' she asked.

'Like a fraud,' I said, 'even though there are bigger frauds in here.'

She looked confused, and so I pressed my point.

'I couldn't make head or tail of the collection, and I don't think a month will make much difference. I was expecting some cursory ceremony, not a Spanish version of Beatle mania. I can't understand why so many journalists are interested.'

'I don't think you realise how famous Valdez is in this country. And in Barcelona – amongst some he is like a symbol for the city. Vibrant, outspoken. People take his legacy very seriously. Plus, all this is a story of intrigue, isn't it?'

'In what way?'

'Famous author leaving a young talent to complete his masterwork. My grandfather starved the press of information about his family, which just makes them all the more keen to find out what they can tonight. The fact that he left his car on a cliff and that his body was never found just brought even more attention to his life. The wrong kind of attention, perhaps.'

I scanned the dress, the fur. She looked iconoclastic. I wondered if Valdez's whole career had been in service of her fame. 'And what about the attention his granddaughter is getting this evening?' I asked.

Laughing, she nudged my shoulder. 'Are you saying I look okay this evening?' she said, with a smile.

'Of course you look okay. It's a lovely dress,' I said.

'Jude,' she said, 'you make me blush.'

I looked at my feet.

'The truth is,' she added, 'I feel like a fraud too.'

I looked at her. 'Velasco gets a cut of the profits if the book is finished. Doesn't he?'

She grimaced.

'Come on, Maria,' I said. 'It is so obvious that man has no interest in literature. Or in anything other than himself.'

'Is that such a problem?' she asked.

'Well, it makes the whole thing seem a bit pointless. Knowing I am only here to further enrich a corrupt man.'

She looked at the floor. Opposite, a church bell chimed. She sighed.

'That is not the only reason you're here,' she said. 'You're here because a great author deemed you worthy.'

'A work you'll also be paid for?'

She shook her head. 'That is where you're wrong,' she said. 'My family ridiculed his writing and his career – that was what first set off his depression. They said that writing these *stories* was beneath him. Even after he was a bestseller, they said it was a flash in the pan; that no one cared. Even when they saw strangers wanting to talk to him about his work they just dismissed them as cranks. So all this irritated him. He became distant. But I always wanted to know my grandfather. *I* always appreciated what he did. It was only in his last months that I got to know him.'

'Right.'

'I want to finish this book because I promised him I would. He called it 'my legacy'. That means something, doesn't it?'

I nodded.

'It means something to you too, Jude. I know that.'

She placed her hand on top of mine. 'There is only one way through this,' she said. 'And that is if we stick together.'

I turned and looked at her. Her thick, parting lips, the glisten in her eyes as they widened. She leant towards me. I caught a flash of perfume as her hand clasped mine. I felt dizzy – the sharp dash of sensuality was unexpected.

'We'll get through this,' she said.

As I looked up, a taxi eased past. Just before it turned away, I caught a glimpse of Francine, looking at us from the back window with a stony stare.

I had never seen that look before.

A cold sensation told me something invisible had snapped.

14

'I am so sorry about this,' I said, trailing Maria into her flat. 'I shouldn't have given Francine my keys and phone.'

'I can't think where she has gone,' Maria said, taking off her fur stole and placing it on a vintage coat stand.

She turned to face me, and placed her hands on her hips. The recent stress was apparent around her eyes. I realised that her attractiveness was dependent on a subtle lustre that she couldn't yet control. 'Do you think she saw us—' she began.

'She must have done,' I snapped, wanting to add, 'when you took my hand.' But I kept my mouth shut, as I sat on the couch opposite her. 'I'd have expected her to have gone back to my flat,' I said. 'But there were definitely no lights – and no one could have ignored that much knocking.'

'Yeah, you're right.'

She started to unpin her hair. Thick, dark locks poured around her shoulders.

'I am sorry you had to wait in the taxi for so long,' I said. 'But I just couldn't accept she wasn't at mine.'

'It's okay. If I hadn't you'd have been stranded.'

'And I'll pay you back for the fare. I know it is a fair journey and that cab wasn't cheap.'

'Take me out for dinner,' she said, her tone brisk. 'And we can call it quits.'

As I nodded, I felt for Francine. I had made her feel foolish and alone, a long way from home. But as I looked at Maria I also felt flattered I was even in her flat, in the heart of this story with her. There was such a sense of history and mysticism about her that in my heart of hearts I knew I would have struggled to resist if she had tried to kiss me, though I had no reason to think she would have. I could detect, playing on her lips, a hint of mischief behind the seeming exasperation, rather than attraction. 'Well – there is plenty of room here,' she said.

I took off my coat, and placed it on a chair. Maria looked at me, her expression reminding me of Francine's scrutiny. The bright red of the lipstick had faded from her mouth.

'You and Francine aren't in a relationship, are you?' she asked.

'It's complicated.'

'But you're not boyfriend and girlfriend?'

'Not exactly, but...'

Maria waved this away with her hand. 'Oh, please. If you're not her boyfriend then she has no right to go off into the night with your possessions.' Maria sounded defiant. She got up. 'Don't worry about it,' she called, moving into the kitchen. 'In the morning, we can go to the university and get the spare key. At the very worst you'll be without your phone. But you have the Internet at your flat, don't you?'

'That's an idea,' I said. 'I'll Facebook her. Can I use your computer?'

'It's on the desk,' she called, disappearing. 'The Wi-Fi code is on the wall above it.'

As I sat down, opened the laptop and went online I felt my frustration rise, my sympathies dismantle.

'I mean – who does she thinks she is?' I fumed. 'She turns up uninvited to stay at mine just as I'm beginning this new project. She demands I act in this specific way when she has no idea what's really going on, and then when she deems me to have fallen short she makes sure I'm homeless for the night.'

Maria came back in, with two glasses of red wine. She placed them on the coffee table in the centre of the room. 'I'll be back in a minute,' she said. 'This dress is pinching.'

A red '1' in the top right corner of Facebook signalled a new message. It was her:

Jude. I would have given you your stuff back but didn't want to interrupt you carrying on with Maria. I know when I'm not wanted. I had a long walk and a think, and I'll stay at yours tonight but I'll be leaving first thing tomorrow. If I don't see you I will leave your things with your neighbour. I know you think I am always testing you, but I hope you are smart enough tonight to not stay at Maria's. That really WILL be the final straw.

Without thinking, I dashed out a reply:

Francine. I am so sorry about this evening. I got caught in the moment and should not have left you. You are so important to me. I don't know what I would do if you were not in my life.

I left the cursor flashing as I weighed up what else to add. Maria came out of her bedroom, wearing a black silk nightgown. She was barefoot. She picked up a glass of wine and curled up on the couch, her back to me.

'Has she messaged?' she asked.

'Yes. Having forced me to stay here she's now saying I had better not. I don't know what to do. I have to get back to the flat.'

Maria shot a look at me. I noticed that although she had washed her face, she had reapplied eye shadow, and perhaps a touch of lip-gloss.

'You won't get a taxi now and it's too far to walk,' she said. 'Besides – we have no more cash. Are you really okay with her ultimatum? You don't think it controlling to keep you away from other women like that?'

Her almost ornate beauty, with its rawness now exposed, grated on me. I wanted to snap 'stop being so good looking!' It was as if now her looks had done their work they were a simple matter of fact. I noticed the slight shine on the side of her nose, and her drawn expression. Minor flaws were somehow indecent on someone whose beauty seemed disruptively indisputable.

'So what do I tell her?' I asked.

She lifted her glass of wine. 'Just come and have a drink. Emotions are running too high for anything to be resolved tonight. You can fix it all in the morning.'

Years of privilege, with leisurely summer holidays and paid staff, were evident in her languorous tone. I realised I barely knew her.

I pressed 'Enter' on the message, and closed the laptop.

15

The first glass of wine slipped down faster than I expected. Maria sat next to me, her legs crossed, and I found myself intrigued by this multi-lingual personification of the good life. As we chatted she laughed readily. But the drink and drama of the evening also revealed layers she had kept hidden. Any questions that implicated her family drew a heavily furrowed brow, and she'd caress her forehead in a strange motion.

Amongst her countenance I sensed a newer threat. It was there whenever she talked of the book, or of Velasco. The furrowed brow quivered, as if she was ready to break into tears. I tried to probe the subject but found myself skilfully parried by her own questions. The parrying turned flirtatious, and yet I sensed that too was not a confection. She seemed *desperate* to have fun, and she topped up our glasses with compulsion. Whatever the real issue, she was not ready to share.

I leant back. She riffed about her family – Spanish fascists on one side, Chilean farmers on the other. There were lulls and sudden emphases, in which English reflections were laced with Spanish words that she explained, enjoying the indulgence. I could not help but be dazzled by the linguistic display. I realised there were many worlds inside this woman, all of them competing for attention. The daughter, the granddaughter, the academic, the bon viveur. The Spaniard, the linguist, and the society beauty. I realised too, that Francine's judgement of her as Machiavellian had been far too simple. No one this capable would choose the easy route and become Machiavellian. That was the recourse of the untalented. I decided that Maria was being compelled by something. Or someone.

As I stood up and asked for the bathroom she pointed towards a door behind her, to my right, and then she relapsed into silence. Was she sulking? Had she been attempting to do something that hadn't worked?

I walked past her and cut down the hallway. I was opening the bathroom door at the end when I saw it. A crack in a door to my left.

Something drew me closer to it. I checked behind me, and eased the door open.

Every wall of her bedroom had been pasted with blown-up pages of quotes from the collection. A novel had been dissected, rendered as a diorama. Circled words, with scrawled notes in margins, connected to others with black lines. Overlaying that dense network, a lattice of interconnecting coloured strings connected circled words. I found myself holding my breath, my heart racing. What was all this? An attempt to map out his mind?

I could see, in red pen, some words scrawled in the margins in capital letters. In the corners of the room were collapsed piles of papers, infested with string, from discarded attempts.

She was trying to solve who this man was – to overcome her grief by ending the conversation with him. Had she been forced to do that? Either way, she was treating the book as a code; a code she had not yet cracked.

It was cracking her.

Resting against the wall behind the door was what looked like a series of paintings. Something told me not to touch them, but I could see that they were of her grandfather. Had he been more than a grandfather – a surrogate parent? His iconic expression – that of the arched eyebrow and the pensive lips – was reproduced in hot reds and singed yellows. It was as if she was reclaiming him from his public image. Trying to will him back to life through the vibrancy of her rendering. I could only imagine the state of mind someone would be in to produce work of this intensity.

As I withdrew from the room I nearly bumped into her. She gave out a small cry, as a tongue of wine lapped out of the glass and then back into it.

'I'm sorry,' I said, 'but that wall display caught my eye.'

She looked up at me, her eyes burning. They had a fierce green I had not noticed before. As we walked back to the living room I felt emboldened by the wine.

'Look, I know this book is getting to you,' I said, as we sat at right angles to each other. 'And I'm not stupid; I know you are under some kind of pressure to finish it. From Velasco.'

She sighed, and looked away.

'I can also tell you are a person of great ability, and I will help you get this done. Don't worry. But you need to be straight with me right now. What is it he has on you?'

She placed her glass down on the table, leant back in her chair, and looked at the ceiling.

'Okay. My family has huge debts. As a result of where my grandfather's money went,' she said. 'These debts include the tuition for my degrees, which Velasco assured my grandfather he would offer but which he now says was a loan.'

'And?'

'He promised to clear all these debts if I finished the book.'

'And if you don't?'

'He says that he will own me. And that there will only be one way I can pay him off.'

I leant forward. 'What do you mean – 'own you'?'

She cocked her head to one side, and feigned a stripper opening her gown. 'Shall I make it any clearer?'

'Christ,' I said. 'What a piece of work. He must know what your grandfather would've thought of that?'

She cocked her head to the other side. 'Well, he takes the view that he looked after my grandfather's welfare and so I owe him. He thinks my grandfather owes him too.' She looked down. 'It sometimes feels as though I am repaying his debts.'

'Even though he awarded your grandfather's fortunes to spurious causes – while you got into debt?'

She looked down. 'Yes. Even though.'

'It seems pretty clear to me that Velasco exploited his intimacy with your grandfather. I think there could be a good legal case you could make about that, to reclaim your money. The sexual harassment too—'

Her face flushed red. 'How could we get into a legal fight with a man who tied up everything using the best lawyers and psychiatrists? How can we do that when all we have known in our generation is debt?'

The Spanish accent was harsh and pronounced.

I opened my hands. 'So it's simple. All I need to do is wave the book through. Tell him that it is completed, and it was left exactly as Valdez wanted it.'

'I have thought of that, Jude. But he is not that stupid. He, and any decent editor, will then ask why the whole collection reads as an utter contradiction. Why the narrative looks incomplete and what it will take to finish it.'

I closed my eyes. Francine's words, her snap verdict, flooded back to me. For some reason, I was able to remember it word-for-word.

'Then we say that the *whole point* is that he didn't want this collection to be finished by anyone. Even me.'

Maria turned to me, and her lips parted.

Listless, as if transfixed by the truth, I remembered the rest of Francine's verdict. 'We say that by appointing me he was declaring me as the person who could get the *closest* to finishing it.'

She ran her hands through her hair. They were shaking, and for a moment I was sure her body was trembling too.

I sat back, anticipating her reaction. I was sure I couldn't take another moment of drama this evening.

'That's it,' she said.

Maria leapt to her feet, her wine spilling onto the floor.

'That's it, Jude – you've cracked it!'

She moved over, and hugged me. I felt the fragility of her body through the thin silk. Despite its erotic pliancy I closed my eyes, and tried to think of Francine. How she might well have just saved Maria and her family from vicious debt. How she had ensured that I had enough money to get through this, to get through the next months, and back on my feet.

'You are brilliant,' she whispered. I felt moisture spread from her eyes and onto my shoulder. 'Oh my god.'

She held me at arm's length, considering me anew. 'You haven't just saved me...' she rubbed her eyebrows in a pincer between two fingers. 'Maybe I can start to just see him as my grandfather again. And not as this burden. Jude – how did you do it?'

'It wasn't me who cracked it, Maria,' I said. 'It was Francine.'

16

The following morning, I was woken by the sound of Maria closing the door. I awoke, and realised I was topless on the couch, my jacket serving as a blanket. My trousers were still on but my shoes and socks were on the floor in a pile. What had happened?

I looked at the table. An empty bottle of wine and two drained glasses. We had clearly not gone straight to bed. What had we done?

I checked my watch, a jagged rip of pain streaking through my mind. I tried to focus on the time. The digits were strange numbers, made up of faint black shards. It took me a second to understand them. It was 10 am.

Francine.

I gathered my belongings and logged on to Facebook.

She had replied. At 4 am.

Jude, I stayed up and waited for you but I can see you are sleeping somewhere else tonight. I have left your stuff with your neighbour and I am heading off in a couple of hours. Good luck with the book. I know it means a lot to Maria that she keeps it between you and her.

I pushed my hand through my hair. What did that mean? Was she threatening me?

Only hours ago Maria and I had agreed that the code had been cracked. Now the one person who'd cracked it was threatening to pull the book from our grasp.

I bashed out a reply, my mind whirring through the various responses I could make.

I slept alone last night, having tried to get back to my flat. But there were no taxis. I went straight back to the flat after the ceremony hoping to see you but there was no sign of you anywhere. Please tell me you have not left yet? Francine – I need to see you. It's urgent.

A few seconds later; the reply.

So where did you sleep then, Jude?

I screamed. It echoed around the walls. I started typing.

It was too late for me to get a taxi home and I didn't have my wallet for a hotel, so Maria gave me her couch

I pressed Enter, after frantically typing the denial I really wanted her to hear. Her reply was instantaneous.

Fuck you. You and your sweetheart can kiss goodbye to the book.

I started typing:

I know I should have been more sensitive last night but you and I are not

The computer buzzed. A message flashed onto the screen.

THE PERSON YOU ARE MESSAGING IS NOT AVAILABLE

17

I hammered on Kimberley's door. There were a few moments of terrible silence, before I heard distant, muffled movement. A bolt was drawn back.

Her face was pristine – a makeup brush in one hand, a white towel wrapped around her body.

'Sorry to bother you, Kimberly. I need my phone – my keys. It's a bit of an emergency.'

She looked taken aback. 'Sure, sure, come in,' she said.

A couple of open holdalls suggested someone who had just moved in – or who was about to leave.

She pointed to my keys, splayed on a blue cushion like a clump of seaweed. My phone and wallet were next to them. I grabbed the phone and fired it up. A stream of messages from my mother, the constant buzz of new emails. Detailed enquiries from my agent. I closed them all, thanking God for the single bar of battery in the top corner of the screen. I scrolled through the address book, finding Francine's mobile number. I rang her.

Finally, the ringing began – a Spanish dial tone. She was still in the country. I grabbed my keys and wallet and backed out of the room, with an apologetic smile. Kimberley's smile was awkward and confused. As I stepped into the hallway I clamped the phone to my ear.

No answer.

I slipped the key into my door and entered the flat. It was pristine. As Francine's answerphone message began I hung up, and then rang it again.

She was either heading to the airport, or to Velasco's office. I glanced at the kitchen table, looking for the manuscript.

In a sinking moment I realised which destination she had chosen.

The manuscript wasn't there.

The answerphone kicked in, for a second time. 'Francine, please don't do anything you might regret. You cracked what was going on with the book, and I know you deserved more from me. But you should not have taken the book – there is more to this than you know. I need those pages back, right away. I *need* to speak to you – for the sake of our relationship, for the sake of us. Please give me that. Please call me back, right away.'

I hung up.

18

I found myself pacing around the flat. What could I do? Get Maria to find out if Velasco was in his office? But even then, an email from Francine telling him Maria had shared the book would be enough for the damage to be done. Velasco would own Maria. If Maria knew Francine had taken the book she would be finished with me too.

I had to just keep ringing her, I decided. I had to hope Francine picked up.

I couldn't just stay in the flat. Was there some sort of way I could get to Velasco? Convince him to ignore anything he might hear from Francine?

I sat down on a chair, my mind racing. It had been difficult to get even a polite response from him at my awards ceremony, so what chance was there of convincing him about anything? But I couldn't think of what else to do.

I kept calling Francine, as I grabbed my wallet and keys and darted downstairs.

It was a hot, humid day, and tourists crowded the pavements. Clustering around outdoor cafes, gaping in shop windows. I hated every one of them.

As I paced through the quad of the university the campus looked as if it was glowing. The jagged line of buildings was backlit by a vibrant sun. The young, pale receptionist did not speak English, but a security guard lingering by her desk did. Sensing the language impasse he translated for her my need to speak to the vice-chancellor. Nodding, she pointed to a building on the map, tucked in the corner of a quad. I asked if she could call him. Sensing my urgency with wide eyes, she dialled his number.

When Velasco's secretary answered – her greeting a faint noise in the handset – she handed the phone to me.

'Hi, I was given an award by the chancellor last night. I just wondered if I could have a very quick word with him?'

'The chancellor has had to leave town,' she said, her English clipped and precise. 'Something came up a few hours ago, which he had to attend to.'

'Is everything okay?' I asked.

As I expected, the question threw her.

'You can email him, if you like?' she said.

I accepted notepad and pen from the receptionist and scribbled his email address down.

As I walked outside I realised that I was completely disoriented, as well as flustered. What could have made him have to rush out of town?

The phone in my pocket blazed to life. I pulled it out.

Francine.

I prayed I wouldn't be cut off as I answered it.

'Hello, can you hear me?'

There was silence for a moment.

'You said it was urgent, Jude.'

Her voice was low, distant.

'Francine, I need the manuscript back.'

More silence.

'Francine, can you hear me?'

'The manuscript? What are you talking about? I don't have it.'

There was a crackle of white noise.

'Francine,' I said, trying to keep calm. 'You told me I could kiss goodbye to the book. I went home and saw that it wasn't on the table. You know what I'm talking about. I need it back.'

'I don't have it. I know what I said but I was just angry. Look – I am at your flat now. Come back. We'll find it.' She sounded irritated, tired.

'Okay. I'm on my way.'

As I hung up the phone I saw an email from Maria.

I am phoning you in a minute, Jude. It's important.

19

During my sprint through the streets, I felt my shirt start to stick to my back. Never had the pavements been so clogged, the air so dense. I had never been as out of breath as when I rounded the corner and saw the entrance to my flat. Francine – with a white sweater over her shoulders and a pensive expression – was sat on the steps outside.

I jogged the last few paces, trying to slow my heart down.

'Are you okay?' she asked, her face flushed as she stood up.

'I think Velasco has something to do with the missing manuscript.'

'I see what you mean,' she answered.

I pushed my key in the door. 'Let's get up there.'

We jogged up the steps. I eased open the front door. The flat was as placid and empty as before. 'Where else would it be but on the table?' I snapped, racing around.

I turned to see Francine was holding a piece of paper.

'Oh my god,' she said.

'What is it?'

I moved over to read it, as she held it up for me:

Jude, I have your book. I let myself in to use the shower and saw it lying there. Your friend mentioned it was precious. Happy to return it.

On an obviously unrelated topic I do need 8000 Euros off you right away, however. Email me on kjosephinewalsh1992@gmail.com to arrange sending the money over. You and I both know 16k is a bit too much for one person to get to sign off a book anyway. So you'll just be spreading the wealth a bit.

As you can probably guess, I didn't get paid.

Thanks for hot water / Internet.

K

I looked at Francine. She looked at me.

Neither of us spoke, for what felt like a minute. We stared at one another and back at the page. 'This is surreal,' I said, at last.

She nodded.

'So, in short,' I stammered, 'what happened last night has cost me 8000 Euros.'

She looked at the floor.

My mobile rang. I pulled it out.

'Maria,' I said.

Francine rolled her eyes, and moved into the kitchen.

'How can I help?' I asked.

'I'm sorry I left abruptly this morning,' she said, 'but I just had to tell the chancellor that you'd cracked the collection.'

'And what did he make of it?'

'When I started to bore him with all my alternative analysis of the collection he just accepted your verdict on it. But I'm pretty sure part of him was annoyed that he wouldn't have a young student as a sexual plaything anymore.'

'It's disgusting that he even wanted that,' I snapped.

'If it wasn't for the money coming his way I don't think he'd have accepted your take. He said that you would still need to write a forward. Five hundred words fleshing out your verdict in a bit more detail. The volume will be published six months from now.'

'Five hundred words?'

'Not bad for 8000 Euros, eh?'

Francine, catching Maria's voice, looked over at me.

'Jude? I can help you with the foreword if you want,' she said. 'In fact I've had some thoughts. I'd like another look at the manuscript before I forget them. If I could come over?'

My mind raced through ways to stall her, without her finding out the truth.

Kimberley's got her way, I thought.

I met Francine's glance. 'I can drop it by yours first thing tomorrow. I just need tonight with it.'

'I can hold out that long,' she said.

20

That evening I brought myself to contact Kimberley. I reasoned with her, I told her that people with the same struggles blackmailing each other wasn't the way forward, I made my disappointment and anger clear. But deep down I also knew that Velasco, or Maria, could insist on having the manuscript back at any point. Though I feared the former more than the latter I also knew that once the book was published it would be worth far more than 8000 Euros. In fact, it was worth more than that now.

In her reply Kimberley insisted the money was paid in full before she returned the book. As I emailed her, Francine returned, confirming to me in a toneless voice that her flat had been vacated.

Francine and I maxed out various bank accounts – and she borrowed a few grand from her brother – and with the last of the pay cheque the university had given me we raised the money to get the book back. As I transferred the final funds and saw the confirmation page Francine wasn't afraid to admit that the book would never have gone missing if she hadn't given my keys away.

I didn't sleep. How could Kimberley have done that given the fact I'd helped her? I tried to imagine the financial hole she'd have to have been in, and how screwed over she must've felt by the world. I considered contacting the police. What if Kimberley kept the money and the book? Francine, with her face down in the pillow, seemed to have gained some peace of mind from the whole situation. But I hadn't. My mind focused on fragments, and pushed itself down painful avenues of thought. Snatched melodies from Beach Boys songs taunted me.

At five in the morning, a crash of the letterbox confirmed the manuscript had been returned. I opened a heavy envelope to find a tattered 100-page manuscript, and an envelope with 1000 Euros in cash inside it.

There was a scrawled note with it. 'For the hot water,' it said.

In the remaining weeks of my stay in Barcelona, Francine and I fleshed out the rest of our book. We sat at right angles to one another in the sunlit living room of my flat. Emails from my agents, opened during the long, hot evenings when we were sat on the terrace, confirmed that the media storm surrounding the prize had been picked up by the English press. A few journalists got in touch, expressing interest in the story of the English writer who had just completed an abandoned masterpiece.

In the final week of our stay, Francine and I finished the opening chapters of our book. The initial feedback from my agent was enthusiastic – she talked of a new 'crossover hit in the making'. She sent us press articles; it seemed the story of the book was gaining more interest than the work itself. I wondered if Valdez was getting lost in all this. As Francine, inspired by the response, slaved away on the book in one corner of the room, in the other I planned the lecture I would give. My final duty in service of this prize. I had given talks before, but had never been clearer about what I wanted to say. In a way, Kimberley had offered me inspiration. I kept thinking of a saying my grandmother used to tell me. 'Hurt people hurt people.'

By the time of the lecture, I had persuaded Velasco, through his receptionist, to wire over the rest of the prize money now that the collection was with the publishers. Safe in the knowledge that it was not his money he was sending, he had the cash transferred into my account after only a week of hassling. Perhaps buoyed by the impending riches from Valdez's collection, he also organised for the university to pay off Maria's remaining tuition fees, under the guise that she'd recently been in service of the university. Maria's emails telling me this also confirmed that her application for a studentship had been successful too.

I confirmed my cleared balance on my phone on the morning of the lecture. Relieved, I flopped back onto the couch. In recent weeks this hard bench wrapped in black plastic had become an unbidding extension of my body. Francine placed a wide brimmed black floppy hat on her head and, smiling, we stepped out into the early morning heat.

The moment I entered the lecture theatre I could see it was full. All the heads in the room turned towards me as we made our way to the front. Judging from the hubbub every English-speaking student in the university seemed to be in attendance; the rows were filled to the back of the room.

As we moved to the front they all leant forward, following me with their eyes. Press attention from the prize had evidently circulated. Students with editions of Valdez novels held in front of them lined the front rows. Their eyes were hungry. Francine pointed out journalists, cameras placed in front of them like uncocked guns. One or two even photographed me as the two of us looked for a place to sit. With a smile, I realised that the days of under-attended literary events were over. I would always be 'the Valdez guy'. Towards the back I caught sight of Maria, who greeted me with a wave. Her low-cut top revealed rather a lot of a sunburnt torso. I surmised that since having her debts cleared she had spent her time replenishing missed sleep in the sun.

A cool gust from the air conditioning seemed to sweep me onto the dais. Francine wished me luck and leant against the seating stack. It was only after I'd introduced myself to the crowd that I saw Velasco enter, cutting to the front row. As I explained how I was the winner of the Valdez prize Velasco turfed a young student in his way out of her chair with a wave. He took his place amongst the press.

I cleared my throat.

'It is great to see so many students of literature here today,' I said. 'As a student myself, I know about the cost of pursuing an education these days. I know about the debts you all have to incur in pursuit of a career.'

I felt all of the eyes of the room upon me, the press shuffling in their seats. One or two put hands onto their cameras but didn't lift them.

I pressed on.

'I know that many of us have gone to university aware that we are the first generation to have to get into debt to study a subject we love. This is a debt that the older generation did not have to have. Despite this, they have had no problem allowing it to be inflicted on us. They have allowed our loans to escalate, along with their interest rates, while universities have become more about making money and less about the love of learning.'

Velasco shifted in his seat. Francine looked over at him with the intensity with which she had long studied me. Some members of the press consulted one another.

'You might ask,' I said, raising my voice, 'what all this has to do with this collection.' I raised the tattered sheaf of papers. 'A collection left behind by perhaps your country's finest writer; a man who inspired me to become a novelist. Well, what I am saying is relevant. Because the executor of his estate, Mr Velasco, used this university's money to further his own ends.'

People leant forward, and some were pricked into making exclamations.

'He did this to award me a prize that would give me the time to read this collection and deem it complete, as Valdez requested. My favourite author let me decide if his final work was fit for consumption.'

I saw Velasco lean over to a journalist. I felt a bulge in my throat but I forced it down. I looked up at Maria, to see her eyes burning from the back of the auditorium. Everyone in the room now seemed to lean forward, the journalists raising their cameras. Velasco was shaking his head, his eyes fixed on me. I rallied myself.

'You might ask why a wealthy vice-chancellor – a man who owns a Bentley, a string of properties, and who is paid millions a year – might want the university to award me money to finish this collection. Well, the truth is – it is because he gets a cut of the royalties once it is published. Not only that – he exploited the debts of the Valdez family.' I looked at Maria. 'In ways you would not believe.'

The tension in the room burst into open consternation. The women at the back shouted down in Velasco's direction. It was as if they had been waiting years for the opportunity to accuse him in public. They threw insults that made him flinch. But he did not turn and address them.

I turned to the journalists. 'My friend Maria Valdez has emails proving this, if journalists would like to see them. I would like to thank Maria for putting in the hard work to complete this collection. And to thank my girlfriend – Francine – for the support she gave me too. And to urge you all to buy a book that makes it clear once and for all that a story is never completed. The writer just takes it as far as they can.'

The room roared to life. Above the din, I shouted, 'Any questions?'

Journalists leapt to their feet. With his hand over his eyes, Velasco leant back. As did Maria, sat many rows behind him. Her smile pierced the room, a dense blast of vivacity.

I was in the living room of my new flat, in Hyde Park, six months later when I read online that Velasco was under pressure to leave his post.

I had not been surprised to read, in the preceding weeks, that he had resisted the pressure to resign, arguing that he alone could 'guide the university through these choppy waters'. Velasco held out after mass student protests, diving student numbers, and outcry from regulators and the press. When students invaded his offices and demanded he be sacked he used university money to hire security to keep them out. It seemed that there was no situation in which he would consider not being the best person for the position. No protest that tweaked a sense of shame. In photographs that appeared in the press his grin was wide and fixed.

It was only when mothers of the students confronted him, one after the other, at a graduation event that he agreed to set a distant date for his retirement. To, at some point, accept a generous pension settlement. That, and the royalties from the book, would maintain his comfortable lifestyle. Maria assured me by email that a string of sexual assault claims from students would whittle away his fortune in time.

I was just closing the laptop when the door of the flat opened. Francine was wearing a stylish red dress, her pinned-up hair revealing a shining complexion. In her hand she held a sheaf of papers.

'How did it go?' I asked.

'The book's been accepted,' she said. 'It'll be published in the UK, US and Spain next year.' She looked around. 'Our cut of the foreign rights will pay for this place for a good while, too.'

I jumped up.

'And I'll be appointing the translator, if that's okay by you?' she added, with a small smile. For a moment I wondered if she had correctly concluded that the best way to handle a narcissist was to refuse them any attention, the currency by which they measured existence. 'There's already more than enough self-aggrandising men involved in this without me enabling more,' she added.

I laughed, took her by the shoulders and kissed her cheek.

'We did it,' she said, handing me the contract.

Part Two

1

I never really believed Velasco would go to prison. As far as I was concerned, that was not the way the world worked. The homeless man who stole food ended up in prison. The immigrant child who only had the worst assumed of them – they went down; and the system ensured the burden was on them to prove their innocence. 'From him who has not, even what he has will be taken away.' But the vice-chancellor with the gold-plated pension? Not a chance. The institution that had enabled him had entwined their fate with his; they would bully those accusing him, even in an age of social media when any such efforts could be exposed fast.

When the rumours of Velasco's abuse of power started to spread I watched the way the smoke built. In quiet moments in my study I would search for his name on Twitter. The sheer number of tweets denouncing him suggested bystanders were becoming emotionally invested in the story. I noticed it was mainly Millennial's – men and women – that were sharing the stories. A certain strand of people decided it was a conspiracy; any evidence offered to refute that was merely more fuel to their fire, adding complexity to theories which they would never fully share.

Velasco was no longer a fringe concern. This Spanish vice-chancellor had become a symbol for corrupt patriarchy. A personification of a rotting system in which portly men treated the world – and women – as a buffet for them to pick through. Like other high-profile men, Velasco had done this with enough insouciance that he had managed to irk strangers. I wondered what he thought of the online tirades by the younger generation. I imagined him attributing their attention to jealousy, and then giving it no more thought.

I kept a meticulous track of the case. Reading all the news articles that followed it as the story unfolded. Sat in the flat overlooking Hyde Park, where I watched pigeons circle as I waited for the article to translate. Words like 'assault', 'abuse' and 'victim' seemed to remove the gloss offered by well-formatted articles and clumsy translations. It wasn't just the victims' pain that was lost in translation. The injustice itself seemed stylised, read from a well-heated room in a recently furnished London flat.

I would feel a slight pinch in my stomach as the article emerged, a paragraph at a time, from a digital mist on the screen. The memory of the speech I had made about Velasco – which had begun his undoing – had become as vague as a dream. The facts obscured by heroic retelling and vague exaggerations. Even I had started to forget the dry mouth and sheer sense of pomposity I felt as I had said those words.

It was the dream of a man far braver than I, but also a man who hadn't thought through the consequences of attacking a more powerful figure. In the pit of my stomach I knew at some point Velasco would come for me. It was only a question of how.

With each article I read I braced myself for the attack. Whenever I saw the phrase 'former vice-chancellor' I could not avoid the thought that I was responsible for that word at the start of each mention.

Once the piece was translated I sat back for a moment, watching the joggers in the park. I considered the digital load in front of me as if it were a letter bomb that demanded careful unwrapping.

The fact that Francine and I now shared this flat added guilt to dread. Before I had only ever lived in bedsits, or couch-surfed. As an adult I had thought of 'home' as being the vague pile of belongings at the foot of whatever surface I slept on. For the first time I had a desk, and the unburdened lifestyle of an author. If I wanted to take off to some far-flung country to research a scene I could. Yet this wasn't proving a comfortable experience. Amongst the cool chrome surfaces of the flat and the pristine white walls I felt like a guest who would not be able to settle the eventual bill. But, as far as I was concerned, it was a leap of faith Francine and I had taken together, and going together into an uncertain future seemed somehow more noble than going into one alone, which seemed merely reckless.

In each of the articles I read, sat in the same spot at my desk, Velasco held the same line. Whether it was a commencement speech, a keynote lecture, or the unveiling of a university building the local press would take the opportunity to confront Velasco with questions about the numerous claims made against him. Short videos embedded in each story would show him smiling in the face of shouted questions. His smile did not falter. I would pause the clips and examine his expression. I could detect no strain on his face, no sign of pallor beneath the tan. If anything, he appeared more relaxed than ever, more capable of not twitching in response to shouts of 'rapist'.

In the evenings I would play the clips for Francine and she would translate the audio for me. 'The journalists are shouting, "What about the women?"' she said. It was a phrase I got used to hearing in Spanish. It was a phrase that haunted me.

'What about the women?' Whether he was being confronted at the university or at some local event, later relayed to national papers, the women remained absent. More and more articles described Velasco using 'pastoral sessions' in his office to offer young, female students preferential accommodation. As he had become more embedded in his role he had used it to offer young women visiting lecturer roles.

The articles established a certain modus operandi. Whether the women consented to his offers or not, each of them reported how he would tell them he was a 'powerful man,' and that they 'wanted him on their side'. He would then turn a departing hug into a forced kiss. One account described him forcing his 'acrid, cigar-tasting' tongue down their throat before assaulting them. One woman – who appeared so young that she must've been almost underage at the time – recounted in a video how he raped her despite her being in tears. Each claimed that he'd warned them that telling anyone of their encounter would end their careers.

At that point I shut the laptop and asked myself why I was getting sucked in.

As the number of cases against Velasco built it all became farcical. Any event he was involved in became a circus – an attempt to get a man who refused to accept reality to at least give it some attention. Despite shouted accusations, stage invasions, loud protests, and despite his car being hailed by missiles, Velasco's demeanour remained the same. He offered a smile or a dismissive wave of the hands. The smile remained the same – broad, toothy. He never deigned to answer questions from his accusers, or to go along with the narrative they were building in any respect. He refused to validate their distress by answering them. It was a deeply infuriating tactic but what was so enraging was that it was working.

However angry you felt over stories of his abuse, he sucked the air out of them the moment he publicly reacted to accusations. The narcissist credo, as ever, was 'I am utterly indifferent to any narrative other than my endless, self-referential one'. His attitude was that the whole circus was an utter irrelevance – a slander made with no shred of evidence. In his mind *he* was the victim. These women wanted a payday, or they were jealous at having missed the opportunity to enjoy his lifestyle with him.

I wondered how Valdez would've reacted to this situation, had he been alive. His characters had been *too* sensitive, *too* easily bruised by the world. How had he ever come into Velasco's orbit – let alone become his friend?

It got to the point where every event Velasco was involved in was besieged with angry students. Only then did the university

1

issue a statement distancing themselves from him. It was shortly after that, once they had finally removed his safety net, that the legal cases began in earnest. 'We are travelling a long road,' said the lawyer of a Joan Suarez, in an article that appeared in the English press. 'But I won't rest until Velasco ends up in prison.'

In lieu of a sense of a mystical hand of justice, this was all we had. The firmness, force and persuasion of human beings, contesting to overlay their narratives with another.

But Velasco seemed to have enough money to absorb any threats; at least for now. He had fixated himself onto the teat of some public money, and it kept flowing. The legal battles began, strangely enough, on the day Francine returned to the flat after a key meeting with our agent.

The door slammed, and I heard her exhale with relief. As ever, I was hunched over the computer. Less immersed in developing my own writing as I was in scrolling through the eight – slowly loading – articles I had minimised at the bottom of my screen. Something made me close the laptop as Francine came into the room. Her cheeks were rosy from what I imagined was a brisk walk home through the park.

'Have the hardbacks arrived?' I said, spotting a package under her arm.

Looking at her, I was surprised by her appearance. The tousled, rough-and-ready façade she had once had – with scuffed shoes and shapeless dresses – had changed since Valdez's last collection had topped the bestseller lists. The chequered dress – revealed as she peeled off her red mackintosh – looked designer.

'Right here,' she said, placing the brown box, wrapped in string, next to my laptop. 'It arrived at Andrea's this morning.'

I had long been convinced that Francine picked up on anything I kept from her. The slow manner in which she placed the article next to my laptop appeared to be a hint that she had noted me closing it.

'You'll never guess what,' she said.

'What?' I asked.

I weighed up telling her about Velasco, but decided she would find my preoccupation with him morbid.

'Andrea just commissioned me to write a new book. Says she has three publishers interested, and they'll all pay advances.'

She threw herself down on the half-dome white plastic chair in the corner. I heard my laptop power down.

'That's brilliant. What'll it be about?'

Her eyes danced. 'It'll be like – an investigative book. The *real* story behind Valdez's demise.'

I leant back in the chair. I had to admit, I had long wondered why there had been so little interest in Valdez's final, reclusive years and his disappearance. It had always been a mere footnote in his story, something salacious enough to bring a touch of intrigue to a story that I felt didn't need it, given the quality of his work.

'So they want you to write about how he died?' I asked.

'Well – given we have no body, the real question is "did he die?"'

I sat up straight. 'What do you mean?'

She was smiling now, running trembling fingers through her hair. The tips of her fingers were red from the cold. 'So we know the trail ended with him being seen, by a local, on the cliff that his car was abandoned on. But no one ever found a body. Did they?'

'True. So what do they want you to write?' I asked, weighing my tone.

She leapt to her feet as she moved over to my desk, before turning and starting a sharp circle between it, and her chair.

'She wants me to examine the details of his final years – in particular his last days. The strange arrangements he made with his family and' – she nodded towards the laptop – 'Velasco. Then to uncover the story behind his disappearance. There is lots of evidence that he planned to disappear.'

'Lots of evidence?'

'Well yes, Jude. There was the closing of his bank account. There was all this money that's still unaccounted for.'

Her tone had sharpened. I decided to acquiesce.

'So they want you to write a book presenting the case that he is still alive?'

She clapped her hands. 'That's it.'

'Wow,' I said. 'That's exciting.'

'Exciting?' She charged over to my chair and sat on my lap. I could smell coffee, and perfume I recognised as Andrea's. I pictured the excited discussion in her office. Francine feigning apathy while inside her keenness built into frenzy. She was used to bookish, theoretical breakthroughs and the delayed gratification of a realisation. But not the excitement of a foregone conclusion – however shaky. 'Andrea says that if I can build a strong case that he is still alive then the interest in his work – and our book – will go through the roof. I've got to tell you – it's been amazing seeing the sales figures that last collection got. But it never really felt *mine*, you know? I will finally have my own project – my own baby. Jude – I think this can be big.'

I wondered why I hadn't been consulted on this book. Francine and I had collaborated on assembling Valdez's last collection – even if cracking it had been her achievement. I had decided to co-credit both of us on the cover, and we had split the generous royalties offered by the contract, after Valesco's cut. We had written the foreword together during a few glorious, sexually charged evenings. Given the physical nature of those days I had assumed any further work on this man would warrant another collaboration. This news took some adjusting to.

I decided to focus on her excitement. I felt undeserving of this new lifestyle anyway; as if it had been bequeathed by Valdez out of perversity rather than accomplishment. I knew I wouldn't even be in this position without Francine's input. I hadn't forgotten, either, what had happened when she had felt threatened by Maria. If she felt this was her big shot then I was going to focus on being happy about it.

'I'm so proud of you,' I said.

She leant down and kissed me. The embrace felt familiar, encompassing.

She turned, leaving a light whirl of perfume in her wake. I detected from the back of her, and the tracing of her hands through the air as she walked, that she was already planning opening chapters.

I turned and opened the string on the parcel. As I did, it occurred to me that I had expected the hardback copy of Valdez's last collection to have rather more bulk to it.

It wasn't a hardback. It was a first edition paperback of the book, the type my office was already filled with. There was a long slip of paper inside the front cover. I pulled it out. In large, printed text the words:

I AM TAKING EVERYTHING OFF YOU. THEN YOU WILL KNOW.

I felt a chill shiver down my back. I turned it over. The other side of the slip was blank. When I turned the slip back over, it roared the same words at me again.

'Can I get you anything?' Francine called, from the kitchen.

2

We had a light supper. Despite the enormous Lebanese meal we had ordered, and the expensive Cabernet Sauvignon we had cracked open, the table was still bursting with barely dented food in foil tins. Cooling flatbreads, curdling sauces and flat surfaces of rice sat like various continents on a sprawling map. The book, with the note tucked underneath it, lay waiting on my table like a bomb. I had always known my unease about exposing Valesco would one day detonate. Now that day had come I wasn't keen to destroy all the trappings Francine and I now had; however conflicted they made me. I had eaten in a slow, pensive style that had suited her sudden reflectiveness. I knew that all Francine wanted to do was fling herself into her bedroom and start typing. I knew that feeling, and admired it. We exchanged a sticky kiss and I returned to my laptop. To the minimised articles.

To my surprise, there had been a development. Five new articles in the last two minutes.

I wondered for a moment if Velasco's abuse was somehow connected to Valdez's death. Somewhere at the back of my mind I was forming the idea that this emergence of his character would reveal a dark truth. It reminded me of my unease about Kimberley – how I had been not entirely shocked when she had blackmailed me. She had threatened an ultimatum and then said; 'What are you going to do about it?' She had done this with the implication that many had done it to her and that it was natural. Velasco seemed to have honed this attitude to perfection.

The first new article took longer than usual to translate. The title took me aback:

VELASCO REFUSES TO STAND TRIAL, CLAIMING DEMENTIA, it roared.

I scrolled down.

Marco Velasco, the Barcelona vice-chancellor who manages the estate of Alberto Valdez, has been besieged by claims he exploited his position at the university to abuse women. Thirteen women have now claimed he offered them university accommodation, only to turn what seemed like charity into an opportunity to sexually abuse them. With the university having finally denounced his behaviour it seemed as if the alleged victims would get their day in court. But this evening Velasco's lawyer, Andrew Cunningham, issued a statement: 'It is with sadness we have to inform the public that Velasco is suffering from an advanced form of dementia.' Asked if this will affect his ability to stand trial, Simon answered; 'Clearly.' More to follow...

I snapped the laptop shut.

3

We cut right off Tottenham Court Road, down a small alleyway. I had never been invited to a book launch before, let alone as part of a couple. Francine clutched the invite embossed with our names as we walked down the staircase, to the basement.

A woman with a streak of orange in her hair unclipped the velvet rope for us as we stepped down into the dim-lit semicircle. The club was filled with bodies. Men in cravats buttoned and unbuttoned their suit jackets, glasses steamed from the chatter. Women in patterned dresses too lurid for daywear tottered in heels too high for the office. The fabric of their outfits was crisp enough to reveal they were being worn for the first time. The women's expressions were pensive, absorbent. I experienced a visceral thrill as Francine took my hand and we stepped into the throng. I felt as if all eyes were on us, but in reality it was the corners of the women's eyes that had become a concern.

In that moment I was acutely aware of the chic cut of Francine's dress, the lustre of her hair, and the way a lock of it was twisted over her shoulder. The women seemed to note all three, and come to hidden conclusions. I was conscious of Francine's slight pout, plump and expectant, as she led me by the hand through the throng, past women holding champagne flutes to their faces. She had considered each aspect of this entrance and her slight smile suggested delight at the outcome. I had never felt part of a glamorous couple before; I had never been led into a crowd. I had never been deemed worthy of sly consideration. With a whisper, Francine suggested we move to the drinks table. Like an absurd camp of two, we clutched champagne flutes as if they were life preservers. Agents who had never replied to my submissions, who I recognised only from portraits on their websites, greeted me as if I was an exotic dancer who'd just turned up at a church ceremony.

Francine and I sipped as we watched a blushing male, decked in tweed, being introduced by a petite publicist. The crowd tightened in a rapt semicircle. I spied amongst the throng expressions that suggested taut admiration and postponed, envious tirades.

'Jude and Francine.' A rich, feminine voice preceded a hug from Andrea, who embraced us into her purple silk dress as if we were her bear cubs. I withdrew, but her hair mingled with Francine's as she hugged her. Black and purple streaks, dry and wispy, entwined with Francine's locks. 'You two make a beautiful couple.'

I had never heard her use that word before, or that louche tone. 'There are so many people dying to meet you,' she said, pushing us into the mob.

A few hours later a strip of amber passed over Francine's face as the taxi accelerated onto the dual carriageway. There was a hint of a smile playing upon the corners of her mouth. It excited and unsettled me.

I remembered first meeting her and thinking how powerful her potential was. Her intellect was so fierce, her perceptions so sharp. I could see that with a little cultivation the world would lie prostrate at her feet. It had also occurred to me how it wasn't for me to stoke the fire of her potential; merely to glow if I got to warm myself on it. Francine had cultivated herself with the rapidity of the destined. However delightful it was to behold, I wasn't secure enough not to feel threatened at times.

Without warning she wrapped her arm around mine and pulled herself into me. I kissed her on the head. As I searched her hair for more of this fragrance I wondered if I was responding to mere chemistry, or if I would be searching for that fragrance for the rest of my life. As she leant back there was a shift in her demeanour. Where the Francine I first met would have slouched, and glowered, she now seemed to revel in a sense of poise. I imagined it spiralling up her spine. The new black coat had a finish to it that glowed under the luminescence of passing streetlights.

The flat was warm when we entered it. The expansive windows that opened out onto the city bathed the lounge in a projected, glacial light. It was as if the city was processing itself, within its own unreadable arrangements. Calmed by the onslaught of darkness. Francine dropped a new handbag – its gold buckle small enough to suggest someone still embarrassed of disposable income – on the glass table. She threw her coat over a wire chair. As she turned to me and opened her arms her smile was fresh. It was the smile of an amateur bon viveur. It had a curl to it – the sense of one embarrassed at life's riches and of the thought of pleasures to come. As we hugged I wished I could photograph her or film the indefinable sequence of movements that I identified as quintessentially *her*. It is a sequence I had barely dared hope would one day frame her in my eyes. In turn, I defined it as a picture of hope.

I moved into her arms, finding her cuddle less wholesome than I had anticipated. We stepped, an awkward four-legged creature, over to the couch. She exhaled in pleasure as I sat on her lap.

Francine tousled the hair around my ear. Looking at her face I decided it was one of shifting expressions. Somewhere under the amiable features elegance was coming to the fore. It created a burn in the pit of my stomach so exciting it dizzied me. Before I knew it I was kissing her with ferocity. She responded with this erotic sob that I hadn't heard before. She bolted upright, unbuttoned the back of her dress and as it fell – a crisp negative of her chest – she looked aware of exposing her cleavage to the London skyline. My shirt was half-unbuttoned as she led me, by the hand, to our bedroom.

That evening all she had talked of was the book. She riffed about places to visit, and archives to uncover. I thought how she seemed to have persuaded herself Valdez was alive; she'd willed him into being by force of conviction. The amateur shrink in me had wondered if she was willing herself to life. My attempts to play devil's advocate were dismissed as mere theoretical sparring. I tried to dismiss the nagging thought that the intellectual rigour I had always admired in her had been blunted by recent validation.

She collapsed on the bed, bouncing a little too high on the thick white duvet. I remembered a line I said to her, as we waited for the taxi: 'A little success dampens the lust for achievement.' I was proud of the line at the time and I admired it in my mind.

I pulled the rest of the dress from her hips, her thighs and calves. The tights on her feet sparkled under the dimmed lights. When I crawled on top of her and kissed her she wrapped her legs tight around me. I felt as if we were in a bubble that I didn't want to break. I wanted to keep kissing her until I understood her, even if it took all night. When our bodies clasped together she smiled and it broke into a laugh, and she smoothed the skin on my neck. 'It's good to be home, isn't it?' she whispered, as if savouring some cosmic joke, and then she kissed me. It occurred to me that this sex was more about celebration than chemistry. Her body had become a tool that amazed her with its dexterity. Her mind had become a circus that impressed her with its sensuality. All the features she considered a burden – her hair, her skin, her figure – had become portals for her brilliance.

Afterwards Francine's body curled onto its side, her hair splayed like sun, the sheets rippling like early morning sand. Her sleep looked fitful and I was jealous of it. I stood over her for a second, as I arranged my shirt around the small of my back. I wondered if she knew the enormous power of her body, of our union, of what we were unleashing. I had always been proud of her rigorous intellect and suspected we would need its rationality now more than ever, just as I feared it was becoming unmoored.

Like an abandoned conspirator, my laptop sparkled on the desk of my study. I realised the paperback – about which Francine had not enquired – was lying there, the slip of paper glowering between it. I placed it behind my folders.

The night sky behind my laptop was obscene in its blackness. Like a sleepwalker going through the motions, I found myself googling Velasco's name. My fingertips tingled with morbid compulsion. I felt myself tense. I was bracing myself for a fight with my own fears. I needed to know what lay ahead; what depravity my adversary was capable of. It felt essential, preparatory. The headlines screamed at me through the night's limp silence:

VELASCO ABUSED ME IN UNIVERSITY CHAPEL, CLAIMS FORMER STUDENT

Frustrated by pop ups and sudden blares of unprovoked adverts, I flickered through the text:

A new alleged victim of Barcelona chancellor Marco Velasco has joined the voices of scores of women who have brought the academic's reputation into disrepute. Velasco, who is also estate manager for Catalan author Alberto Valdez, faces claims that seven years ago he offered to take an eighteen-year-old prospective student on a tour of the university. Emilie Sierra, now of Madrid, claims, 'He took me into the university chapel, having persuaded my father to take a tour of the library. Even though there were other people, including some nuns, in the chapel, he took me into a quiet corner of it. He placed a prayer book over his hand and looked over my shoulder. I will never forget what happened next. He let the book fall to his lap and then he touched me. When I tried to shout out he clasped his hand over my mouth to stop me screaming. I could not believe no one saw or heard. Or that no one tried to help me. It was surreal.' Sierra then goes on to describe how the former vice-chancellor raped her in the university chapel.

I found myself scanning the end of the article:

Alleged victims of Velasco have expressed anger that his impending trial has been delayed on account of a dementia diagnosis. Sierra commented; 'Every day new information about Velasco's disgusting abuse of power is coming to light, and we were starting to hope that we might – at long last – see justice. We find it very suspicious that this is the moment he has started to tell people he has dementia. It seems very convenient that as a result he cannot attend a trial. Put plainly, we believe his political affiliations are protecting him, along with the personal wealth he can use to hire the best lawyers.'

Another, unnamed, alleged victim added, 'Velasco has treated us with contempt from our first encounters with him to the present day. He was fit enough to undertake a lecture tour two months ago but he now claims he's unfit to stand trial. This doesn't surprise me. There is no depravity to which this man will not sink. Take it from me.' Velasco, and his lawyers, declined to comment on the claims. They instead referenced the last press release citing the diagnosis of dementia.'

I realised my eyes were bulging. Sore with the strain of reading the text on such a bright screen.

'Jude?'

Francine's voice echoed from the bedroom. I closed the laptop. 'On my way,' I called.

'What are you doing?' she asked, as I entered the room.

She was sat upright in the bed, her fringe thick over her face.

'I was – reading some articles.'

'About Valdez?'

'Velasco.'

She threw the fringe over her head. 'I sometimes feel like we are living with these men too. Like they are inside me.'

I did not know how to react.

'Jude?'

'Yeah?'

I thought for a moment of our bodies mixed together, of how inextricable it felt.

'Do you promise that's what you were doing?'

'What?' I asked. 'Of course that's what I was doing.'

Nothing else came in the post for the next few weeks.

I assured myself that at worst Velasco had my agent's address, but that over the Christmas period we were safe. Each morning I wondered if another parcel from him might be waiting the next time I visited Andrea. But I also told myself that Velasco might not even have sent the note. I spent days considering the ambiguity of the words on that note. What did he mean by 'THEN YOU WILL KNOW'? Whenever I resolved to share it with Francine, her exuberance seemed so fresh it seemed sadistic to spoil it.

The issue of where we would spend Christmas was floated by her, and then addressed just as fast. We were at the dining table making the most of a French breakfast – composed of pancakes and croissants – when the subject was raised. I realised this was how Francine handled ambiguous issues. She devised courses of action and then opened conversations knowing where they would go. I started to wonder what plan she had in mind for us, now it had been agreed she would stay at my parents for the season.

During the early days of our friendship her own family had never been discussed. But pressed in against each other in train seats she told me about her childhood. She'd been the product of an affair between her mum and her married dad. Her dad had denied her existence until having to admit to it when her mum was wheeling her in a pram and she physically bumped into her dad and his wife when rounding a corner.

I noted, in the use of the terms 'the daughter' and 'the dad', someone who had come to think of herself as a mere character in the drama of her own life. Was such a displacement the way in which she'd willed success onto herself? Was it also the reason she assumed Valdez was alive? One departed father figure had not been dead, but merely displaced through their own will. Their corruption something that could be investigated, overcome.

It was only when I saw Francine step into the station car park to greet my mother – a blizzard of blue fur stoles and padded coating – that I realised I knew little about this woman. My recent preoccupation with Velasco had distracted me from enquiring about the person I was living with. I was under-appreciating her, thinking of her as part of a lifestyle. I promised myself to address that.

As Francine stood in the kitchen my mother served us a feast of baked salmon, quiche and roast potatoes. Her hands inverted on her hips as Francine stood behind a chair and chatted about her recent book deal. She hinted at joint investment plans for us, which I knew nothing about.

It occurred to me that you could get permission for physical intimacy with someone but you would still be shut out from the mental compartments they dwelt in. My mother's eye fell to details of Francine with all the louche attitude of a forensic detective. I saw her take in the dry tips of Francine's hair, and mentally assign appropriate conditioner. I saw, as we ate, her note the heavy eyeliner and consider it an attempt to balance out a shade of foundation that, though expensive, was not quite correct. My father – a man waiting with admirable patience for half-moon spectacles to come back into fashion – questioned her on her book. During the exchange my mother scrutinised her without words. After a long debate she spoke up.

'Well, all that matters to me,' my mother embarked, 'is that we have a new addition to the family.' She raised her diet lemonade. The bubbles fizzed and popped. Looking at Francine I saw an expression of relief, belonging and satisfaction. 'To Francine,' she said.

My father's smile was raised for longer than his glass. 'Oh,' he said, rubbing his hands on his turtleneck. 'I forgot – a parcel arrived for you.'

Francine looked over at me.

My father went to a chair in the corner of the kitchen and handed me a small brown box. I felt the heat fall from my face. 'I've been wondering what this is,' he said, adjusting his glasses.

'A new edition of Valdez's last collection,' I said. 'I told our agent we'd be away and asked her to post it here.'

Francine's gaze snapped to me, knowing every part of the sentence was a lie. She resented the confidence with which it had been delivered; I could see that.

'Let's see it then,' my mother pressed.

'Let's finish dinner. No more work,' I said, picking up my cutlery.

'Jude,' Francine whispered, picking up her wine. 'Bit rude, no?'

'It's okay,' my mother said, sensing the rising dynamic. 'I know what you high fliers are like. I can scarcely believe it. My son, with his brilliant girlfriend. Writing bestsellers about huge international dramas they are at the heart of.'

'There's more of the story to come,' Francine said. She looked at me with a smile, and then placed her hand on top of mine. 'I like to think we're just getting started.'

I placed the parcel on my lap. Francine watched me do it, and then turned to smile back at my mother.

5

Amongst the whirl of board games, savoured whiskies and cooling coffees, the parcel wasn't mentioned for the rest of the evening. Having placed it next to me on my chair in a manner that was entirely unnatural I went from the living room to the kitchen to open it. The hubbub of my parents' phatic communion became a distant echo. Looking over my shoulder, I opened the parcel.

Another copy of the same book, another long white slip. I anticipated the scream. This time it went:

YOUR GIRLFRIEND'S BOOK WILL MAKE HER A LAUGHING STOCK. THE MORE SHE DIGS THE MORE YOUR LIVES WILL UNRAVEL. THEN YOU WILL KNOW WHAT ITS LIKE.

For a moment the dropped apostrophe on 'its' caused me some doubt. Would Velasco have missed it, even in his second language? What about the lack of the words 'for me' after 'what it's like'? Was he ensuring an impartial observer would not assume his involvement?

Hearing movement, I folded the slip and put it in my pocket. Francine emerged, holding a glass of wine. 'I've come for more red,' she said. She looked at the book. 'Christ, Jude, you look like you've seen a ghost.'

I opened my mouth, but no words came.

'So why do you keep getting sent paperbacks of Valdez's last collection? What's going on?'

I had dreaded this conversation. I could hear my parents laughing. The relief in my mother's voice spoke of years of worry. The suspicions that her son would never make money, never make a name for himself, never be in a secure relationship – all wrought in that sonorous note. The memory of past struggles discussed within these walls, when the type of life I now had felt like fantasy, rendered me mute.

'I don't know,' I said. 'But it's freaking me out.'

Her mouth made a small 'o' of sympathy and she wrapped her arms around me. I closed my eyes, and thought of the disappointed look on my mother's face when rejection letters had arrived at the house. A house I had been too poor to leave.

I wanted to wrap myself in the veil of Francine's perfume, in the slender embrace of her arms. I refused to allow myself to do anything to end that feeling. Somehow, deep down, I knew I was on borrowed time. That I did not deserve all this. That soon the sanctuary of Francine's mind and body would be gone.

I wanted to tell her what the note said. But I suspected that would begin the ending. What hurt me most, as I bunched my fist into the paper in my pocket, was the thought that Velasco knew all this too.

6

Over the next few days Francine was caught in a whirl of activity and we barely spoke. With a bitter stare from the kitchen she noted my keenness to intercept the post. On one occasion, when I pushed past her to get a fresh pile, she snapped; 'Even if it's another few paperbacks, what's the big deal?' Having rifled through the pile and retired to my desk I took in the steam rising from the pavement outside, mingling with the early morning mist in the park.

At that moment in time I knew two forks were open in the road for me. I either told Francine and shared my fears, or I managed them alone, as I had always done. Any doubts I had about taking the latter path (the former felt unremitting, dark and jagged to me) were eased by the sense of lightness Francine emanated. It was there in her loose hair, livened with new highlights. It was there in the open-necked light blue and white shirts she had started to wear. In the bracing smell of the cooking I returned home to after my evening walks. It was there, as well, in the sudden digressions of her speech, as if to her life was now shimmering with possibilities. If anything, the darker accusations of secrecy she made towards me only strengthened my resolve. I felt as if I was taking care of business.

The letter came the following day. I recognised the Spanish post stamp, and was relieved that Francine passed no comment as I withdrew to my study. I realised that the embossed, thick envelope was not Velasco's usual style of communication. I pulled out a note, written in lush italics:

Dear Jude,

I hope you don't mind me writing but I wanted to tell you how deeply grateful I am to you. Not only for your cleverness in finding a way to finish my grandfather's last collection, but also for the way you used your position to expose a man who has tyrannised my family for many years. Most people would've simply taken the money and flown back to England. You used the opportunity you had to tell the whole world what he had done. I hope you feel proud because as a result of this he is now finally facing legal consequences. It is not just me who has been able to step out of his shadow as a result of what you did. In some ways, and I know this sounds so silly, but I feel I owe my life to you! Or a new lease of my life at the very least. I was so buried in grief for my grandfather, that the pressure to complete the collection was driving me crazy. No one will ever know the toll it was starting to make on me, nor do I want them to. I wanted to complete his book to feel connected with him, as if I finally knew him. Yet I was also under huge pressure to complete the book so Velasco could not control me any longer.

You pulled me out of that situation.

I don't know if you have had the chance to follow the story of Velasco's case in the press. Even if so, you would not have been able to learn what is really happening. Yes, it is encouraging that so many women are now testifying against Velasco. But Velasco is strong, powerful, and he is cunning. His claim to suffer dementia, sadly, is convincing people. It uses their sense of empathy against them. You may not know it, but amongst his victims you have become something of a hero. But they disagree on so many things, such as how to fight him and whether to seek damages. I fear that their lack of unity will allow Velasco to evade justice. Just as he always has done.

I must admit, I was not writing just to thank you. I was also writing to ask you one last favour.

I think if you were to appear at his first appearance in court you will help bring the victims together. You will inspire them to solidarity. Jude, please come.

On the back of this letter are the details of his court appearance.

Regardless of this, I want you to know that as you were there for me, I will be here for you.

Always,

Maria.

I exhaled, and placed the letter under my laptop. As I did so, I reached into my top drawer and pulled out a notepad and a pen. Seeing Maria's impassioned words had roused something in me. It felt incredible to think I might have made a difference in this story.

Looking back it astounds me to think how that moment might have been the high point of my life. It was a brief moment in which I was making a name for myself, in which I had a brilliant partner, and when I had a plush apartment and money. Yes, I had a sense of guilt and unease about it all but those positives were all there. Yet I reached out for my pen and began writing to Maria as if what happened next was inevitable. When I know now that it was a choice.

I remember what I was thinking at that moment. I see myself from outside the glass, looking in on a worried man settling at his desk. In a matter of months I had won a prestigious award, and had helped finish my favourite novelist's last work. I had exposed a man who had caused much suffering. But after the years of refusal and frustration, I just knew I would not resist playing the role Maria had cast me in.

I wrote:

Dear Maria,

Thank you for your letter. It is hard for me to describe how powerful your impact on my life has been too. Before the award, and before you and I worked to complete that collection, I had felt useless, side-lined. I think the rush of empowerment I felt during that stay in Barcelona made me feel that anything was possible. I have to thank you for that feeling. Of course I will come out and join you. I

I heard a bang behind me, and my name being called out. I pushed my letter, along with Maria's reply, under my laptop.

'Yes?' I said, standing up. I felt conscious of the ridiculous campness of my tone.

Francine appeared in the doorway. Her mackintosh looked as though it had been thrown on as she was leaving a room. Her face was flushed; a lock of dark hair was stuck to her lip. In that instant her face seemed somehow ludicrous in its roundness, as if a revelation had skewed her enough to reframe her in my eyes.

'Are you okay?' I asked.

'Something's come up,' she said, placing her keys on the desk beside my laptop.

'Something good, or something bad?'

'A diary. Left by Valdez, in his university office.'

'A diary?'

'He apparently thought he'd lost it. He'd complained to many people that it had been stolen. But in fact he had dropped it down the back of his desk.'

Her clinical tone was hiding something, I decided. Something important.

'So I'm guessing this diary revealed something?'

'I don't have it yet, but a woman who worked in the department with him found it when she moved into his room. She looked me up and – can you believe it? She emailed my agent today. To ask if I would find it interesting.'

I tried not to react to the use of the term 'I'.

'And what does this diary say?'

She brushed her forehead with the back of her hand, and took off her coat. 'It's full of plans he had for moving abroad. It looks like he was thinking of starting a new life in another country. Using another identity.'

It took a few moments before I realised that my silence seemed like an insult. But I had been trying to fit the pieces together in my mind. The notes I had been sent had made it clear Francine was wrong to think Valdez had survived. Yet this diary suggested otherwise.

'You don't look very happy for me,' she said.

'You don't seem happy either,' I retorted.

We moved into the living room. I leant against the wall. Francine threw her mackintosh at the kitchen table, before she sat at it. As I settled opposite her I tried to work out what it was about her that revealed such agitation. She started chewing on her finger, a gesture I hadn't seen before.

Her eyes flashed at me. 'Jude,' she snapped. 'I have to ask. Is it professional jealousy that's stopping you from showing me any kind of excitement for these developments? Or are you hiding something?'

I sat opposite her, and took her hands. 'Francine, believe me. No one is more pleased to see you getting the success you deserve. Without you having cracked Valdez's last book I'd be nothing. I suppose—'

'What?'

'I suppose I just want to be certain that your book is going to argue something that is true.'

She leant back. She exhaled, in a long breath.

'I see. And is there any reason for you to be so negative? Do you have any solid evidence that Valdez is dead? Like, I don't know, a body?'

'No. I suppose—'

'Which returns me to my original suspicion. This is professional jealousy. You have no problem taking my support when it's in service of your own success. But when I need *your* support...'

She had practised this speech. The clauses were too tight for it to be improvised. Her cheeks were burning red.

'Perhaps a trip to Barcelona would be a good idea,' I began. 'To gather the evidence?'

She sat bolt upright.

'Now why would *you* be going back to Barcelona?'

'I'm not saying *me*, necessarily. I'm saying that leads are all great but — solid evidence. That is what is really needed. Before you put your name on the line.'

Francine stood bolt upright. The chair banged onto the hard floor. 'I am not the one whose name needs working on. I have a book on the go, and a commission. A high-profile story. You are still dining out on a breakthrough *I* offered you.'

'Francine—'

'No. Fuck you, Jude,' she said, smacking a hand against the chair and moving to the door.

'Francine, come on,' I said, blocking her path. 'Don't do this. Look around you.'

I leant in, and saw the frantic breathing she was trying to calm. It was rippling through her body in a way I had never seen. I knew something was being pushed to the surface that had been bubbling for a while. I cupped her cheek in my hand, desperate to control it. Her face was hot.

'Look at the life you and I have started to build. We have to stick together.' I waved a hand around me. 'We can't lose all this for the sake of … suspicions. You and I are in this together.'

She looked up at me, her eyes burning. 'I need to be alone, Jude. Do you get it? Alone.'

'Well where do you expect me to go?'

'To the pub. To the park. Try and find yourself a friend.'

'Come on—' I reached out my hand. She pushed it away. 'No way,' she said, recoiling. 'I'd rather throw myself under a bus than continue this conversation with you.'

I blanched. 'Francine, don't talk like that. We're on this journey together. If you did something like that – my life would end as well. It'd be pointless. I need you.'

'No, you don't. You don't even want me: you're bored of me.'

I leant forward. 'That's not true. How could I ever be bored of you? You're smarter than me; you're more ambitious than me. I love you.'

In the rush of the moment I'd expected those words to fix everything. When she shook her head it shook me to the core. I saw tears squeeze from her eyes. 'You have this idea of what you want to be, and I am just an accessory to that,' she whispered. 'When we break up, you'll understand what I mean.'

I felt my eyes bulge. '*When* we break up? Whoever said anything about…'

She held up her hand. 'I need to be alone, Jude. Will you give me an hour alone in this flat, without me having to feel tense around you? I need a bath, and something to eat.'

'Are you serious?'

Her hands tensed. I saw veins ripple up her arms.

'*I want to be alone!*'

The scream shook the walls and the glass. They shuddered in shock. I moved to the table. Picked up my keys.

Francine was shaking.

'Fine. I'm going,' I said.

7

For the last month all I had thought about was Francine's note.

That night I'd returned home to read Francine was leaving me. There was no opportunity to try and prise off her sense of resolve. She had made her decision and she was clean away. I was helpless.

From that moment my life was placed on a new set of rails. Those rails took me into a new emotional territory – where the ache of waiting and a corrosive sense of resentment were everpresent accomplices. As I boarded the train to the airport those feelings travelled with me.

Sat on the train, my suitcase wedged above me, I closed my eyes whenever we entered a tunnel. I told myself that the noise was a cocoon, wrapping me in a protective layer. Since Francine's departure I had felt as if a layer of skin had been peeled from me.

Coming back after that walk I had been horrified to see she had cleared the house of her possessions. A discarded suitcase tab was the only trace of her.

She'd been nursing something alone and it had cut so deep that she'd felt unable to share it. I suspected it connected with the insights she'd offered about her parents, but it wasn't for me to say for sure. All I knew was that she'd chosen, without any time pressure, to end our relationship through a note rather than make herself vulnerable enough to have that conversation.

Francine's note had gouged a wound that had become more infected with time. Those hastily scrawled words had become a pet injury that I tended to in each moment. Each time I had to pay a bill for the flat I'd been left with the scar was torn open. In a single moment I was left alone with the life we'd set up together. I'd had no warning of what was coming. There were days when leaving the house I'd feel a pain so acute that each step felt impossible to complete. It was as if oxygen I'd taken for granted had been removed.

The reason she had given, as I reminded myself each day, was that she felt 'too insecure in the relationship'. But because of arguments we'd had she 'didn't want to tell me in person'. Three lines into her note came the damning words – 'I found the letter from Maria, and your reply to her. It is obvious to me you are planning to cheat on me with her,' she wrote. 'So I am giving you the freedom to do that. Don't contact me. You will only try to talk me into thinking I'm wrong. I'm not going to give you the chance to do that, Jude.'

My parents, shocked at the course my life had taken, had assured me that if someone was going to act in such a dismissive way then they weren't truly ready for a solid relationship. My mother, in particular, asserted that 'anyone who ends a serious relationship in a phone call, a note, an email, a WhatsApp message – you deserve better. It's poor of them. If they aren't mature enough to honour the intimacy of what the two of you shared by discussing the end of it in person, then frankly they've come up short. It's not like you'd put her in any danger. She owed you more after the journey you'd begun *together*.' But somehow, no matter how often she recited this, her words hadn't helped.

As the train approached the airport I went over events for the thousandth time. The days after, when I had sorely hoped for a call from her. The days after that, when my anger coalesced into acceptance that someone I thought I knew I had not known. How I had then nurtured the vain hope she would come back and return her key. I had felt unable to call her; I was stunned at how she had handled her departure. What would I say if she picked up the phone?

As the weeks went on, and I heard nothing from her I had to accept the likelihood that I would never hear from her again. The bills for the flat had been in my name, and I wondered for how long she had had one eye on a sudden departure. Had she set up our living arrangements in case she one day wanted to bolt? She hadn't returned a key, and every night I had lain in bed half-expecting the click of the door. This anxiety, this half-a-breakup, extended to me expecting something reconciliatory, something more, whenever I turned on my phone. But there was nothing but a digital void.

The train entered another tunnel, slewing into pitch darkness. But my thoughts did not relent – they had stayed with me day and night for the last four weeks, after all. Even when I tried to block them out they continued their incessant chatter, the questions burbling away in my mind. Had Francine ensured there was an almost invisible lino beneath our life that she could yank out if she wanted? I cursed my naivety. I had thought that shared experience and shared plans were protecting me from this outcome.

When I didn't hear from her I held out hope that Andrea would offer the chance for reconciliation between us. When I visited her in her office I somehow thought the key to understanding the breakup would be offered to me. But, when prompted, all Andrea said was that Francine had 'dropped by' to mention the breakup, twirling her thick dark hair around her finger, a smile on her round, catlike face as she added that it was 'sad but inevitable'. I pressed Andrea for more details, feeling more exposed as I did so.

She told me Francine had mentioned she was 'working out how to proceed'. When I asked what this meant, with a lowered brow she told me she 'didn't want to get involved'. There was a moment when I reflected on the absurdity of the intricate way she was folding and unfolding her fingers. Even when she had a strong financial incentive to help us overcome a misunderstanding, all this effort was going into studiously avoiding helping, her eyes trained on her lap. I could not believe her nonchalance. It was another layer of security I had been relying on – that those who made money off me cared for what was best for me – that I now realised only existed in my mind.

At that moment in Andrea's office I reclined in my chair, and realised I would have to look elsewhere for answers. Francine and I weren't married, and so when she had moved out there was no enforced reason the severance wasn't complete in that instant. On the night I'd left the flat and gone on that walk I'd had no idea I was closing the door on a whole life.

At the airport I tried to force the bitterness from my mind. It had been well over a month and there had been no word. But as I left security, switching my phone to 'Airplane' mode, I still wondered if I might be about to miss a call from her. If I might now miss out on a long-awaited explanation.

Given her accusation regarding Maria I had debated whether or not to go to Barcelona and support the women. But the fact remained that there was nothing keeping me in England now; only a flat aching with memories. I knew that my secretiveness had intended to protect our life together and not rouse a paranoia and jealousy from her that I had pretended I was not familiar with. I was aware that if I spoke to Francine I would've only vented my frustrations at her and that wouldn't have been fair. I would have admitted the challenges I had offered our relationship by being secretive, apologised for my shortcomings. But I also would have insisted I did not think that excused the way she had left. Even as I boarded the plane I played the same script over in my head, and wondered if I'd ever get to read it for her.

By then I knew the lines of argument, and the lull in energy that followed their mental articulation. The practised barbs I had planned, for if we ever spoke. As the plane lifted off the runway I knew something else too. That Francine leaving had placed me on a path leading me towards the events to come. At that moment my dinner with Maria that night had a grim inevitability about it. If it became romantic it would prove

Francine's reaction to be valid. And if there were a distinct lack of chemistry between Maria and I then my sense of absurdity about the whole situation would only be heightened. I was flying into a lose-lose situation.

In truth, I had tainted the meeting with Maria in the month leading up to it. I had revealed myself to be a changed man, my confidence damaged by the breakup, and this in turn would affect how she saw me. Between consoling phone calls with friends, and intense attempts to clear my brain of my anger and confusion, I had exchanged a few brief messages with Maria.

But my current state of mind – at once lonely and yet quick to temper – came with its own consequences. Maria's initial relieved and friendly tone became more and more laboured as I tried too hard to keep the correspondence up. I should've known that a month of corresponding with someone would exhaust the fragile sense of intimacy that had flickered between us. If Maria wondered whether I was capable of rallying Valdez's victims in my current state then she kept any doubts to herself.

I'd once mentioned what had happened to her. My last few messages to her in the days before I got on the plane had gone unanswered. It is a bitter irony that in the moments in life when you are most lonely you are most unattractive to people. When you exude confidence and charisma people admire you for it. But when you need your energy and inspiration the most you find yourself spent. What I wanted to say to Maria was that I had never been more driven to help bring Velasco to justice. When I had read those articles again, in preparation for the trip, it had been the raw sense of injustice that had started to make me feel alive again. But my twisted logic also told me Valdez had provoked the breakup. His threatening notes had started the secrecy, had fuelled the bonfire. Maria had just offered the spark. I could've admitted Maria's letter and Valdez's notes to Francine. Part of me knew I should have done, and that I'd been irresponsible. But another part wondered if doing that would've still led to the same outcome. Valdez had created a situation intended to unravel my life, to enact revenge on me. In turn, what I most wanted was for him to pay for that.

This preyed on my mind as I walked onto the rooftop terrace Maria and I had agreed to meet on. As I looked for her, I wondered how much she would guess the degree to which I was teetering. She would be hoping I had the stomach for a fight, yet I knew I was close to mental collapse after so many agonised nights. As I looked around me, past the sunburnt diners, I tried to rally myself. Despite the breakup, I still had my career. Maintaining a good relationship with Maria was key to that and, if she could offer me any solace, I knew it would soothe me. The restaurant was full – crammed with dining couples exchanging careful chatter. Barcelona was a compressed tapestry of red, caramel and grey in the distance. The wails and moans of the city seeped up from below us.

'You made it,' she said, appearing from nowhere.

I had forgotten how piercing her eyes were contrasted against her dark hair, how embarrassing her beauty was. I found it unreasonably confrontational in its insouciance. Her black dress became an elaborate lattice between her shoulders; it clung to her figure as she kissed my cheek.

Her sparkling mouth formed a reserved smile. A waiter pointed out a table on the edge of the terrace, and we sat opposite one another. The evening sea was just visible, a margin of blue beyond the ochre city.

'You look well,' I said. 'In fact – you look a little like you are on holiday.'

She pulled a face – part confused, part amused. We ordered meals from a waitress, who poured us both a glass of white. Maria squirmed in her seat. I imagined her making love to an undamaged Spaniard.

'Getting Valdez to face his victims is far from a holiday,' she said, reaching for her glass.

'Of course,' I answered, 'I didn't meant that.'

She re-considered the wine menu. 'It's okay,' she said, tapping my hand. 'You've been through a lot recently. Are you sure you're ready to face him in court?'

'You have no idea how ready I am.'

'Hmm.'

'That man has unravelled so many lives.'

Her gaze suggested she thought I needed a weekend at home. I steeled myself. I was not going to let this opportunity pass. Not for me – or for the women.

'I'm wondering whether we should've ordered a bottle,' I said, feeling the sheer desperation seep from my pores. I knew I was transforming in her eyes; from being the saviour to being a pathetic wretch.

I sat back in my chair and took in the marble sky. It was amazing how quickly a change in tone occurred between people. In her letter Maria had come across as devoted. One sudden breakup later, and now her words were irrelevant.

I felt my resentment rise. She was just using me to get what she wanted. I leant forward and I wondered if I was so different. Was I dining out on her beauty, thinking I had some right to bathe in its glow?

'Velasco sent those notes to unsettle me,' I said. 'What infuriates me is how delighted he would be to know how effective they were.'

She nodded, and cradled her fingers together. In the flicker of her eyes I saw her dismiss various responses before fixing on one. 'You should channel your anger into helping his victims, Jude. Maybe all your hurt can be useful. Maybe you can use it to ensure that their testimonies are as powerful as they can be?'

'And that's why you want me here?'

The question felt like a dig. It occurred to me that her and I had never been entirely straight with one another.

I sensed in her eyes a calculation taking place. Her expression suggested she could see I had few options. I could feel my assumed power fade away, and with it went her respect and benediction.

'Of course,' she said, turning over the menu.

It stung to hear her admit that was the only reason I was here. I looked over at the sky and reminded myself that my feelings were not important. It was all about the case. 'I won't let you down,' I said.

'I know you won't,' she said, in a singsong voice. 'You wouldn't have come all this way if you were going to let me down.'

I felt too angry to nod at the remark, borne as it was of fresh contempt.

'We can discuss the case after dinner, Jude. But regarding ... what happened to you. I just want to say one thing. Even if it is not my place to. Would you mind?'

'Why not?'

'Okay.' She leant forward, and the sun caught the line of her cheekbone. 'Okay. Well – I never liked Francine.'

'Oh?'

'Jude, you must've noticed. She seemed so resentful of me. It was so *undignified*, all that sulking. She seemed to want to remove anything female from your life; you really think that's healthy?'

I loved the unashamed passion she was exuding.

'I am sure you have made lots of women jealous, Maria.'

She twitched at the compliment. There was still a flicker of something there and I wagered all it would take was another woman showing an interest in me to foster it. 'All I am saying is, you can't base your life around someone who will leave you like that, without even doing it face-to-face. When might they do it next?' She waved her hands in the air in a most Mediterranean way, satisfied with her conclusion. 'She obviously had locked something up inside herself that she was refusing to share. This was all just a matter of time.'

I thought of my mother's advice. 'You might be right.'

'And because she thought you were about to cheat on her! With who?'

Her gaze focused on me. I wilted under its pressure and felt the heat of the evening.

'*Aquí tienes*.' A waitress placed the linguine and the Greek salad down on the table.

'Don't worry about it,' I said, as she left. 'Because I wasn't going to cheat.'

A vulnerable look passed over Maria's face. It pressed on a bruise inside me. It was a reminder that to other people any injustice you experience is at best a curiosity. Francine had a key eye for the realities of human engagement and I wondered if she intended to maximise the hurt as much as possible.

I picked up my knife and fork, and dismissed the thought as ridiculous.

'One day you will meet someone who can't bear to be parted from you,' Maria said. 'People don't always know how much they are hurting others. Or they lack the maturity to care – all they can experience is their reactions.'

'People sometimes forget they're not the only ones feeling pain,' I said. How much time had I spent thinking about my breakup, when a huge miscarriage of justice was looming: one that would go down in history? I was appalled by my rampant self-pity, so far down the list of the woes people had. I'd got out of something seen as unhealthy by rudimentary observers; how was that bad?

'That's only human,' Maria said.

'But that doesn't make it okay,' I answered.

As I started eating, I had the strange sensation I was filling a void inside me. Maria watched, barely picking at her own food, and I sensed in her eyes the type of analysis I had undertaken of her when we first met.

8

I felt a chilling sense of intimacy with Velasco as I saw his victims gather inside the courtroom. As I approached them a mere glance demonstrated Velasco's sexual preference, and seemed to prove his guilt. All of them were blonde, wide-eyed, and their expressions hinted at trapped traumas. It was only as I drew closer that I saw the nuances of their personalities and attitudes, once the superficial attributes Velasco had pursued fell away. They were clustered around a door that I could not see the significance of.

I sensed Maria's empathy as she guided me in their direction. She introduced us to each other in fluid Spanish, the names the only details I could retain. The various geometries of closed bodies and faces altered to let me into their midst, with varying degrees of warmth. I had never been more self-conscious about being a man, and yet Maria's reminder of my role in exposing Velasco seemed to validate my intrusive sense of righteousness.

I was introduced to a Lucia – a mousy blonde, with a triangle of freckles on her nose. 'You did us a great service,' said the more confident Francesca, an icy blonde with sharp incisors. An older woman named Melinda surveyed the pack with a sisterly air. 'We are going to get justice today,' she said, jabbing a finger as she addressed the women.

'Anything you want to say?' Maria asked, leaning into me.

I gulped. Maria's expression teetered between anticipated disappointment and hope. 'Most of them speak English,' she added.

Get over yourself, I thought. I nodded at Maria, working myself into a state of conviction.

'There is something I want to say,' I said, turning to them. I raked a glance across their demeanours, glad that it collected their attention. 'This man,' I said, pointing to the entrance of the court, 'has had everything his way. All his life. However well you do today,' I said, encouraged by the rise in Maria's shoulders, 'he will delay, deny and hide from what is coming to him. The best chance you have of seeing any justice done towards this man,' I said, lowering my voice, 'is to testify with such passion that no one can be in *any doubt* that you are telling the truth.'

Some of the women placed reassuring hands on one another's backs. Others nodded. I thought of Velasco's letters, and felt my anger rise.

'Make *everyone* want to do *everything* they can to put this man in prison.'

'Yes,' Melinda growled. To my surprise there was a smattering of cheers. Amongst the hurt and confused eyes I saw some sparkle.

'He's arriving,' Maria said.

The courtroom doors opened, photographers backing through them. Cameras flashed and a man fell onto his side. With the blast of cool air came a further tide of people. A retreating throng that didn't look like it would break. Amongst it, the familiar bulk of Velasco – a horrid shock in grey designer coat. A lawyer was holding up his elbow, with dramatic deference, as if he was fragile enough to fall at any moment. As the shouting journalists parted I glimpsed his smile. It cut through the horde, unabashed and proud. He looked as if he was about to cut the tape on a new leisure centre.

'*Bastardy*,' Melinda hissed. A few of her accomplices joined the cry. As he drew nearer they turned, recoiled. He acted as if they were not there, with such conviction I wondered for a moment if they had vanished. This is what men like him do, I told myself. Acknowledge what they want to acknowledge; turn threat to an advantage. As if to prove my theory Velasco bowed to hostile journalists like they were autograph hunters. The chatty Spanish of his wiry lawyer suggested confidence that the case was being thrown out. I heard a word that sounded like 'dementia'. It was repeated with the intensity of an Arabic prayer, a panacea to cure all Velasco's ills. It felt a bizarre mantra.

'What a piece of work,' I said, as he approached. I felt an angry coldness shimmer through me. Velasco did not seem to recognise me, his glazed look drifting past. I was convinced at that moment that he could not have sent me those notes; that I was not worthy of his consideration. But a moment later I realised this was the kind of disconnect he had engendered in people for years. You attributed motives to him in his absence, but a moment in his company dragged you into his version of events.

As he walked away I was able to see the whole story. His sense of entitlement over these women's bodies. His belief that their claims were beneath contempt. I saw, as well, his ability to turn furore to his advantage. His whole career now made sense to me.

The women were shaking. Francesca started crying. Melissa put an arm around her. I felt as if I was struggling to breathe; that I was out of my depth.

Maria took my elbow. 'Well, you did what you could,' she said.

9

In the court we braced ourselves, the voyeurs and the victims, in a delicate conspiracy of anticipation. The charade of Velasco's entrance gave events a sense of momentum. At the entrance to the court his lawyers held him up as if fearing a second fall – when none of us remembered the first. When Velasco picked his way to the dock it was as if he had never navigated a room before. But at one point he stopped, looked around himself at the gallery and announced; 'Maravilloso.' I felt my fists clench in my pockets from my seated vantage point. The solipsism of the narcissist, their pride insisting that only their own judgement mattered, in case any observer dared think they might be evolving.

Despite my unfamiliarity with the language I felt a low thrill when I heard him give his name. It seemed to energise the women, who tensed. I thought of a consolation goal scored by a team who had already lost the match. He gave his name, as if bemused by the favour being extracted from him. The women looked at one another and steeled themselves with sharp intakes of breath.

The debrief afterwards, in an annex of the courtrooms, unpacked little of the hearing. I detected from the rapid Spanish that the women were making the most of any glimpses of discomfort seen on Velasco's face. I was unconvinced. My first brush with legality had left me hollow, aware of the need to look elsewhere for a sense of justice. Velasco had dismissed even the fact that he had been dragged to court. I found my way to a distant, marble finished bathroom. I tried to convince myself that his nonchalance was an act and that he was hurting inside. But the fact I had seen no evidence for that made me want to scream.

I was washing my hands and trying to slow my heart when a cubicle opened behind me. Velasco was walking away from a flushing toilet, all trailing scarf and surging stomach. I saw my eyeballs widen in the mirror and felt a cold shiver knife down my back. As he leant over the washbasin next to mine I took in the overpowering, almost sensual scent of aftershave. He looked down on me, lips curled. I regretted my crouching position.

'You,' he said.

I turned, and felt a need to grab him by the throat.

His voice was rich with past cigars and planned rebukes. 'You, who would condemn a dying man,' he said, squeezing soap from the dispenser onto his leathery hands.

I stood upright. I told myself I would replay this exchange in years to come.

'You're not dying any more than I am,' I said.

He let out a reluctant growl.

'I notice you don't need your minders to visit the toilet, then?'

He laughed.

'You think you are so familiar with my story?' he growled. 'You think you know about Valdez? Just because you got a few charitable Euros from us?'

He leant forward and washed his hands. I tried to work out my next line of attack. But my pause gave him confidence.

'You know nothing,' he said. 'You're just another grave robber.' He turned away from me, and dried his hands on a towel. 'You're just like those women out there. Those *parasites*.'

'You abused those women,' I countered. 'One look in their eyes proves it.'

I was frightened by my anger. The last time we had spoken I had been currying his favour, but now it was the sense of snatched opportunity that was driving me; that, and the thought of future regret. 'I know all about how you threatened Maria.'

He didn't react to her name.

'They all wanted something from me,' he replied. 'As I did from them.'

'So you admit that you —'

He interrupted me with a swat of his hands. 'You English are such cowards. Hiding behind theory,' he said, scrunching up the towel and throwing it into the sink.

He faced the mirror and adjusted his shoulders. He looked around himself, with an expression of almost theatrical cunning. 'I tell you this, as a dying man who knows you will never be able to prove it. Alberto Valdez killed himself.'

I recoiled. What sick game was this?

'Oh, the English man is surprised,' he said, addressing a non-existent crowd. 'Yes. I saw Alberto throw himself from a cliff. Into the North Atlantic Sea.'

He seemed to relish the vowels of 'sea'. As if he was imparting some biblical knowledge.

He took in my stunned silence. 'Oh yes,' he said, adjusting his bow tie. 'We went there for a walk on the beach together, after he came out of the hospital. We were talking about his struggles. I was trying to *help*.'

He viewed his own hands in disgust, and then looked at me as he took a deep breath.

'I went back to the car for something and in a moment of impulse he did it.'

He gauged my reaction, and seemed to find it wanting.

'I saw it.' He sniffed. 'I will take it to my grave. A moment which is not so long away.'

'So why are you telling *me* this?'

'Because of what you did to me. You want to ruin my life's work? Then I will do the same to you.'

On 'you' he jabbed a fat finger in my face. As it drew close to mine I felt his foul breath on my cheeks. It smelt of cigars and unbroken sleep.

'I know you and your girlfriend think you can make a living by hunting for Valdez,' he growled. 'I am telling you what happened to him to take that from you.'

I tried to feign incredulity. 'If that is true why have you allowed people to believe he disappeared?'

'Out of *duty*,' he said. 'The one way to make sure his books keep selling is to make sure the mystery is never solved.' He looked around himself again, before lowering his voice. 'And you will never be able to prove what I just told you. But you'll still know it.' His gaze levelled with mine. He smiled.

'So the question is – do you tell your girlfriend? Do you ruin the meal ticket?'

'You know what I think?' I said, drawing close to him. I could sense no fragility in his body, no suffering. 'I think you killed him to make money. I think you're telling me this to ensure no one else gets the spoils.'

He smiled. 'No, you don't. You know I am telling the truth. The question for you is, do you keep it to yourself?'

I felt something collapse on top of me. I felt emptied. As if I'd been turned inside out.

The door opened. I was glad to be interrupted before he saw my reaction, though I knew that for years to come I would regret that moment. What else might fate have revealed to me if the door hadn't opened then?

It was the wiry lawyer, reeking of desperation. He took one look at the situation. The body language, the palpable tension. His eyes bulged in a way I found grotesque. 'Mr Velasco,' he said, taking his sleeve. 'We have to go.'

'That's okay,' Velasco said, pulling away from me. 'I'm done here.'

10

Velasco died four months later.

The news left me mute.

The interim had been a strange lacuna, a void of inaction. A gulf in which various schemes to try and help me move on from Francine came and went. They all failed, with varying degrees of intensity. To deal with the space she had left behind I had, on impulse, taken in a lodger.

She had come to a book event of mine in a local book shop and stayed on to chat afterwards. I'd been unnerved by the heavy annotations she'd made in my novel, and I had made a misguided attempt to pay back her commitment by offering her my spare room when she mentioned struggling to find a residence. I'd naively thought that as a result of this decision there'd be at least one person in my life not keen to disagree with me.

It was her who had given me the news.

Taking in Lily had been an odd strategy, attempted as a band-aid. I had heard nothing from Francine in those four months – no amount of delays in checking my mobile phone granted any further explanation for her departure.

The kind of author events I met Lily at had been accepted in the hope they'd distract me. Amongst the frightening array of readers and aspiring writers, with their varying motives and degrees of sincerity, Lily had stood out. She had an almost comic sincerity. The pale, slightly round face that I came to decide was grim in its beauty. The yoga pants, paired with trainers, which I couldn't quite reconcile with her pea green overcoat. In the Q and A after she retained the air of someone just keeping hold of a hilarious secret no one else knew. It was during the socialising afterwards – which she entered with exaggerated nervousness in the book shop café – that she mentioned her impending eviction. I thought of the useless space in my flat and casually offered her the spare room. In her deep brown eyes I saw trembling relief. I was surprised by the reaction. Behind her gaze I had detected a hint of sweetness, and some parochial boredom. When she accepted the offer without pause I realised I didn't know her at all and had just let her deep into my life.

She told me about Velasco after a desultory morning of writing. I was reaching into the fridge for the milk, and from Francine's chair Lily looked up from her laptop and asked; 'What do you think about Velasco dying?'

I looked at her but no words came out. In the absence of anything to say I poured myself a glass of milk. I thought of the last few months, in which I'd tried to come to terms with my confrontation of him. I had told her this story at least twice – and now he was gone.

'Says here he died in his sleep,' she said. 'With a smile on his face, no doubt.'

I knew she was provoking me, a trick she had recently developed to draw me out of my silences. On the day she moved in it had been clear to me that under usual circumstances Lily would make the most of the awkwardness of living with a man. But desperation had raised her level of tolerance, and in the process she'd developed some new tricks.

I tried to hide the pain this news left me in. I decided my laptop would offer some answers.

When I googled Velasco's 'news' it was there in black and white – in an article bordered with an advert:

A source close to the former vice-chancellor revealed last night that he had died at his home in Barcelona. He is survived by his wife, Marie-Elena, his daughter Carmen and his son Anton. Velasco had been suffering dementia, a diagnosis that had caused significant controversy after a host of allegations were recently brought against him. Joan Suarez, the lawyer representing Velasco's alleged victims, commented: 'This news comes as a significant blow to my clients. The fact that their abuser died peacefully in his sleep while they are left to piece their lives back together is hard to take. We will be pursuing this case through various compensatory processes, but I would just like to make one point. If people had believed these women when they first spoke out, and if the university had not protected a serial offender for so long, justice might have been achieved while Velasco was alive. I leave it to others to decide whether the claims of dementia were genuine or a delaying tactic that worked well for him.' An alleged victim of Velasco's, Melanie García, added, 'Velasco only gained fame and riches because of his dubious friendship with a famous author. But this friendship protected him right until his death. It is a source of daily agony knowing that vile man will never face justice. Some of us are comforted by a belief in a wider justice but we should not need to default to it.'

I snapped the laptop shut, and closed my eyes. I thought again about the urgent conversation I had had with a lawyer friend on the phone, moments after arriving back in England. While leaning against the pillar in the airport lobby I had told him what Velasco had revealed to me. Amongst the sound of fading signals I had caught my friend's memorable reply. 'A boast in a bathroom doesn't prove Velasco was guilty, Jude. Not in a way anyone would take seriously. You need enough evidence to persuade a jury.'

I stood up, and started to circle my study. In that moment I realised something. I alone knew what had happened to Valdez. It was quite possible Velasco had only told me the truth about what had happened to him.

I felt weighed down by this knowledge; it was as if a building had collapsed on top of me. I felt a crushing sense of responsibility. Every time I read an article speculating on Valdez's whereabouts it was quite possible that I knew something no one else did.

I had never felt such a sensation before. I was at once chosen, and cursed.

In the months since my return I had weighed up whether to try and get in touch with Francine. Whether to tell her that I knew the answer to the great mystery she was dedicating her life to solving. I had to now admit that Velasco had convinced me. But I also wanted her to gain a perspective on her sudden fleeing, and to see it in the sharp light of clarity. I knew that me bothering her would not only disrespect what she'd asked of me but also remove giving her that perspective.

But my resentment of her had dashed any chance of me getting in touch. Fantasies about how this knowledge might lead her to regret her departure had consumed me for hours. I asked myself if I was really capable of spoiling her ambitions by revealing what I knew.

As I darted around the flat, deep in thought, Lily looked over at me with a furrowed brow. Before today I had comforted myself that Velasco, in time, would confess to others. But that comfort was now gone.

Since being back in England I had started dreaming about Velasco's victims.

In these dreams I saw their bloodless expressions as they walked back to the places in which they'd been attacked, trying to make sense of the absurdity of denied abuse. The testimony of that student in the chapel had sounded all too plausible. But what use was the truth now Velasco was dead? It was simply now a matter of their word being set against his. With him 'no longer able to defend himself'. Velasco had become a black box.

I went back into my study, sat down in my chair and gazed out at the white sky. We would never know what was inside that black box. Velasco had got away with it. The last time I had seen him he had been boasting, smiling and dismissing. Now he was gone. I put my head in my hands. A sheer sense of injustice throbbed in on my ribcage. *What now? Did I hope that hell existed?* In truth, I did not believe it did exist. I had a passing, flickering sense that in whatever calmer, displaced place the dead went there was more clarity about the consequences of their intent. It was curious to me that I now could sense, as if activated by empathy, the shape of such a place, unclouded as my own judgement was by direct trauma.

There was a knock at the door. Lily opened it with care. She had changed into a white dress. Her expression roused a smile on my face – it was formal to the point of absurdity. As if to enunciate the sense of the surreal she poked a teapot through the crack in the door.

'You can come in,' I said.

'You looked like you could do with a hot drink.'

'Thanks,' I said, gesturing to the empty mug on my table. She poured, the rich steam curling. For a moment it seemed to mix with the mist outside my window. I felt a sense of shame. What kind of man would ask her to move in with him? Someone whose life was a blank page, who took any opportunity to fill it with the first opportunity, sensing something destined about something coming along to fill it. I remembered the relief on Lily's face when I had made my offer.

She looked at the pile of papers next to my computer. 'Is that the new novel?' she asked, feigning nonchalance.

'Uh, huh,' I said.

'Can I read it?' she asked.

I looked down at the pile of papers.

'You sure you want to?'

She stepped forward.

'I'd love to. You know, I cited your novel quite a lot in my MA.'

I wasn't sure how to react.

'Okay. Well, I'll email it now.'

'Great.'

'Why don't you send me something you're working on?' I asked, knowing that she had at least one novel on the go. 'We can trade opinions.'

She nodded, fast. 'I have … something. Yeah, I have something I could send. I'll do that now.'

I turned, opened my inbox and sent her my manuscript. Whatever this novel was – whatever it was going to be – it was now out in the world.

Lily studied me, like a window stain that had appeared out of nowhere.

'You know, it's none of my business, Jude, but you haven't really been out much recently.'

'True.'

'There's a Creative Writing Night on at a uni café tonight.'

'Are you reading?'

Her cheeks flushed red. They were more of a presence than I had envisaged. 'No,' she said. 'But you should get away from your own writing. From your own…' She looked over my shoulder. 'I don't know. Thoughts.' She brightened, with a vivid smile. 'We could even have a glass of wine?'

I thought of the evening I had planned – one of dried noodles, followed by watching the world outside my window grow dark. Then I pictured an oaky glass of red wine, me curling up in the corner of a bar with it. Words whirled around me, hopeless and luminescent; a cascade of fairy lights.

'Good idea,' I said. 'What time does it start?'

'Eight.'

'Okay. Why don't we both take a look at each other's work, and then exchange verdicts as we walk there. At quarter to?'

'Sounds good.'

11

It was strange being out of the house. I wasn't used to walking through the steam that rose off the pavements, or seeing the flicker of the early evening lights in the distance. I was used to the dank air of my own existence, of lying on my bed in the study and trying to clear my head. Trying to work out what'd happened to Francine. The news about Velasco had disjointed something inside me, and it was a relief to not think about it. As I walked next to Lily – her pea green coat replaced with a tight-fitting cream number – I wondered why I hadn't abandoned my obsessions sooner.

Her eyes were underscored with thick eyeliner, and the silver clip pinning up a lock of her hair somehow added to a sense of occasion. I wondered how she felt about the situation. As she evaluated my novel her hands whirled in the air – the nails a shade of deep red that I hadn't before seen on her. I had just decided her dismissal of my stylistic tics was generous when she gave me her verdict. 'The thing is,' she said, 'your novel can't become that great until you know how it ends. How can you know what the story is, unless you know how to finish it?'

'But where does any story finish?' I answered. 'It has certain parts that feel important, and you use a novel to try and set them down. That doesn't mean you have to tie up all the loose ends. That's unrealistic.'

'Well unless you know what happens to the loose ends, how can you write a story?' she countered.

As we got to a crossroads and prepared to cross for the tearooms she stopped. 'So – what did you think of my book?' she asked.

As we darted between cars my mind flickered back to her manuscript. What did I think? I'd liked the sumptuous gothic imagery. The subtle, probing psychoanalysis undertaken by her protagonist. She was talented but I knew that was a word that held a mercurial currency. The boon of making someone feel validated carried the risk that they instantly started thinking themselves the next Tolstoy. I'd seen it a thousand times; talent was sometimes too heavy a burden to place on someone for a sense of self-gratification.

'You're definitely onto something,' I said.

'Really?'

Her face flushed red.

'Your writing is so rich,' I continued, cringing at the abstract lexis I tended to use when appraising fiction. Why was language so inadequate, when tasked with appreciating the inner chambers of a person? 'And it has these undercurrents that to me are really the heart of the....'

'Story.' She flashed a smile as she finished my sentence, impatient to live her life with her talent as the vehicle. As we turned in a new direction her hand grazed mine. It decided to settle on the crook of my arm, touching it for just a moment.

'Thank you, Jude,' she said. 'I was so nervous about what you'd think of it.'

'You needn't have been. My story paled in comparison,' I said.

I could see through the faint distortion of the Victorian windows that in the tearooms a reading was taking place. Candles illuminated the crowd in a warm, low luminescence. The door creaked as we opened it and I realised that the whole of the campus faculty were turning to look at the two of us. Lily tucked a lock of hair over her ear, and parted her shining lips. I looked to the stage.

The readings swirled around me. A story told by a man in a hunting hat pulled me into its slipstream and I briefly lost myself. Most of the stories had potbellied, bearded men in ironic cartoon t-shirts recasting themselves as swashbuckling heroes with swords in a gritty middle earth scenario. In their stories the women tended to be damsels in distress, waiting for a white knight from their halls of residence.

Throughout most of the readings there was a register that disengaged me, and let me retreat into my own thoughts. Why did literary readings all require the same tone – one of bruised stoicism? As the man interrupted his poem every two lines to remind us what stanza we were on I considered his images. Yet another poet trying to convey a weak sense of heroism through descriptions of their mundane hedonism. Were the poems skewering the older generation, or crying out for a better world? All I could hear in these stories about shitty people treating each other in shitty ways was an empty nihilism. Tear it down by all means, but then surely you had to build it back up? So many stories were Irvine Welsh rip-offs. He might've told us we could 'Choose Life'– and that meant consumerism, the other option being drugs. But beyond that binary there had to be something more – people wanting to heal, wanting to create something positive?

I tried to ensure my expression remained one of earnest consideration. From our position at the back of the room, Lily touched my elbow and whispered staccato verdicts of each piece. 'A bit needy' and 'Enough with the daddy issues' were the only ones I fully heard. I suspected she was needling from me the sense that she could calibrate others' writing. In fact, was that all she wanted from me, a sense that I was a validated figure who'd somehow give her a shortcut to the world? I smiled at her precociousness and decided that the scent of cheap perfume and new nylon emanating from her was appealing.

As the crowd moved out of the pub I fixated on the idea of Lily's proximity. I imagined Francine, in the company of some handsome admirer, breezing past us and I decided that the proximity of Lily's charisma would allow me to survive such an encounter with my pride intact.

Perhaps this was how Velasco's abuse had begun? A man being flattered to think some attractive woman still found him attractive, and dining out on it? Had that feeling then hardened, becoming a fierce sense of entitlement as it felt under jeopardy? It was an important juncture of realisation for me to know that no, it was not that. A man like him was carrying a wound I was not, and saw women as material with which to staunch it. I could watch for signs of slippage but they were a different creature.

It was only after an admirer of hers had left, to fight it out in the taxi rank, that Lily turned to me. The scent of her perfume had faded. Now the mild hint of rose in her moisturiser was prominent, invigorated by her movements.

'You know I'm totally grateful you letting me stay, but I have to tell you. You're the worst flatmate ever,' she said, poking my arm with her finger.

I laughed. 'What do you mean?'

She seemed to have practised the itinerary of complaint.

'You always lie and say that you're going to do the washing up and then when I do it you don't even thank me. You mope in your dressing gown for days. You're mute for whole afternoons. Shall I go on?'

'What about you?' I asked, with a smile.

'What do you mean?'

'I see pink delicates on every radiator I turn to.'

She laughed. 'Did you really just say 'delicates'? Wow.' Her smile broadened. 'You like me being there. God knows what you were like before I was around.'

I cast my mind back. To nights spent at my desk, looking out into the dark. The acute sense of rejection on seeing no new messages, whenever I gave in and checked my phone.

'I suppose so,' I said.

As she moved to the bathroom I glanced at her again and thought of Velasco. Perhaps this was how it had all begun with him? An ill-advised moment, on a night when they both felt vulnerable? Was there really a darker pathology in him from the outset?

As Lily left the bathroom I saw she had touched up her lip-gloss, and that the silver hair clip seemed a little higher than before.

'Let's go home,' she said.

12

'You two going to the same place?'

The taxi driver shouted the question. As we got into the cab, the stale air mixed with the fug in my brain to create an agreeable sense of wooziness.

'Yeah,' I answered.

His eyes flickered in the mirror as Lily put on her seatbelt. Her hand touched mine. 'Lucky me,' she laughed. I looked at her and smiled at the raw sarcasm. As the amber margins of passing streetlights lit her face I noticed that the sparkle was still there on her mouth.

'You're going to kiss me, aren't you?' she asked, looking out at the nights.

I hesitated.

The cab driver's eyes flickered in the mirror. He came to some conclusion about the two of us that was imperceptible.

'What's there to think about?' she asked.

I could see the driver's eyes trying not to meet mine in the mirror. I watched the skyscrapers loom in the window, then shrink. In the end I whispered. 'It might not be a good idea.'

'Why not?' her tone suggested she was on the edge of being offended.

'I don't know. The power imbalance? I'm kind of your landlord, for a start...'

'I liked your novel. And you'd need to own the house to be a landlord. And besides, all that doesn't stop you being a man and me a woman. Does it?'

'I didn't say it did.'

I tried to read her eyes in the dark as she spoke. Streetlights streaked across her eyes, bathing them in amber, then red. 'So what if I became a millionaire, and you had lost your job and were homeless?' she asked. 'Would that make it wrong for us to kiss?'

The taxi driver was looking right at me. With subtle precision, he shook his head. As if guiding me towards my answer. Or was he shaking his head in judgement of her? I couldn't tell. But it was odd to have this play out in earshot of him. Surely she knew he was listening?

'No,' I said. 'But I still don't think I should kiss you.'

'You think I should kiss you then? Because I have to tell you, I'm not that bothered either way.'

The taxi driver looked at me, his mouth a little agape. I wasn't sure if he was lamenting her clearly being attracted only to someone who seemed determined to be inaccessible, a projection she could explore something of herself with, or the sense of missed opportunity he perceived on my part.

I looked at her mouth as she laughed. She stopped laughing, and looked at mine.

I knew I was on the verge of taking a fork down a new road. I knew as well that this decision would turn out to be a bad one. Yet the fierce pulse of my heart had made a decision on my behalf.

I turned my head to hers, and she turned her head to mine in the same instant.

The driver coughed.

Startled, I pulled myself back.

'What?' she asked, her eyes moist in the glare of the streetlamps.

'It wouldn't be right,' I said.

~*~

At home, the grim comparison I had made between myself and Velasco was still in my mind, ever present, as I put my keys on the glass table. Lily stepped slowly in behind me.

I thought of the cold night outside, and the lights in the window of the tearoom. I could see in her eyes that she expected the author to have the answer; or at least for him to have considered it. I wasn't prepared to be a staging post in the series of disappointments that would demarcate her life. 'So what happens now?' she asked.

'We sleep.'

13

The next morning I sat down at my desk, took a glug of scalding coffee and wondered if I should look up Velasco. Somehow, the routine had lost its sense of necessity. In the distance I heard Lily pad barefoot around the flat. I resisted the urge to rush outside and greet her.

I texted Maria. The sense of rapture in my body congealed into anger as I remembered the manner of Velasco's passing. Its desultory, smooth quality.

I typed:

That's that then. Velasco got away with it.

A small icon with three dots denoted her replying. She said:

Makes me sick to my stomach.

The icon revealed she was still typing.

His victims certainly feel that way. Even his family do.

I responded with:

How do you know?

Her explanation was already in progress:

I became friends with his granddaughter, Rosalie, after she got in touch with me.

How curious, I thought.

So what does she think of it all? Is she relieved he's dead?

It looked as if she was continually typing.

More complicated than that. Velasco's son (her dad) is sure he was innocent. She seems sure he was not.

I snapped back a reply:

What makes her sure? It must take courage to admit your grandfather abused women.

As I waited for her response I contemplated whether or not Maria would refute my claim. How courageous is it to accept the obvious? Her response came in a satisfying chunk:

I agree. I sometimes wonder if something happened to her to make her so sure. It is tough for her, she has fallen out with her father as a result of what she believes. Maybe because of that, she spends a lot of time at the family's holiday home in Morocco. Says Valdez's archive is there, along with some of her grandfather's diaries. She said 'I feel like I'm in the middle of it and in the middle of nowhere at the same time.' It's like she's trying her best to confront the truth but she also can't quite bring herself to.

I wasn't sure what to make of that. I typed the word:

Interesting.

Maria had more to say:

When I asked what she thought about Velasco dying she said, 'It feels like the best and worst thing at the same time.'

The only sentences I had heard from this Rosalie had been contradictions, I thought.

I typed:

Sounds like she's pretty confused.

Her reply was instant-

Wouldn't you be?

That's it, I thought. Velasco's diaries. The black box. The place where the truth about him resides.

The idea came to me quick as a flash.

Do you think she would let me see Valdez's archive if I visited Morocco? And perhaps Velasco's diaries as well?

The reply was not instant. I watched the screen for a whole minute, twitching in my chair until a reply flashed up:

Maybe.

Then:

Given that you were the one who first exposed Velasco ... who knows.

The idea was taking hold in my mind.

Would you ask? I did fly out to Barcelona!

The brightness of the smiling emoticon that began her reply lifted me.

You're saying I owe you a favour?

I smiled.

I typed:

I could do with a trip right now.

It occurred to me that it wasn't a strong line of argument, but I felt loathe to reveal more. Her reply snapped back:

His diaries might have the one thing his victims need. Evidence. It looks like they are throwing the case out of court unless solid proof of what Velasco did is found. Now he is dead there is apparently no case to answer.

Enraged, I bashed out a reply.

That makes the trip even more urgent then.

The moment I pressed 'send' her reply came.

Really his family should be going through his diaries. She should be. I can understand her feeling conflicted ... but still. You're a good man, Jude. I'll look into it.

My finger hovered over the keys. Did I tell her about Velasco's confession in the courthouse? Something made me resist revealing it. I didn't want to look like a fool if, in Morocco, I found evidence that contradicted what he'd said.

I wondered if it was the thought of Francine that was subconsciously pushing me to go to Morocco? Was I really a good man, or just morbidly curious?

The moment Maria had mentioned the archives I had known I would be getting away from this situation and onto that flight.

14

The moment I stepped off the plane at Marrakech airport the shirt stuck to my back. I tensed.

The flight had been far too emotional to leave me in a relaxed frame of mind. A woozy slumber had slipped into a muggy dream, in which Francine and I exchanged silent glances in a bar. I had dreamt I was on my way to meet her, walking through a hinterland of traffic islands and pedestrian paths, knowing I wouldn't find her.

As I walked into the airport I checked my phone. The tyranny of the blank screen reminded me there was no replacement for Francine, and still no sense of progress on the matter. I had known that changing continents wouldn't shift this emotional blockage, but it was disappointing to see that confirmed. A few messages to exes and to women who'd once been interested had warranted no reply. I put my phone away. All it had taken was a warmly worded letter from Maria and Francine had prised herself from my life. The wound left by this sudden cleave was still gaping inside me.

I waited to have my passport stamped, trying to block out the noise from an argument behind me. I had still heard nothing from her and in the interim my resentment had swollen to fill the gap. Resentment had become an ever-present accomplice. Each pulse of my throbbing head exacerbated the sense of emptiness. It was a feeling that grew worse in busy places. It had become a noxious, black cloud.

Looking around I could see various people with missing limbs, or eyes; people who hobbled when they walked. I told myself not to surrender into self-pity; it seemed to me like everyone was carrying wounds and many were more evident than mine. Making my way out of the airport I caught the heavy sigh of a vendor when a tourist passed them; saw his long stares into the middle distance. Everyone was suffering some kind of pain; I was not special.

As I walked out of the airport a Chinese tourist clattered into me, causing me to drop my suitcase. I was embarrassed by the stares I drew as I collected it from the floor. I stood in the taxi rank, calmed by the shade. Two Arabic men came up to me from the street. Something told me I should begin negotiations. 'Es-salamu alaikum,' I said, remembering my guidebook.

'Salaam,' one answered, weighing me with his eyes. 'Français?'

'Je suis Anglais.'

I showed him the restaurant I was meeting Rosalie at on Google maps. He turned to his friend, and made a joke in Arabic about 'Rue Mouassine', safe in the knowledge I was now relying on a few French phrases for my negotiation.

As he drove I grew accustomed to the elaborate, almost elegant way the driver tapped the hooter, as if it was a delicate percussive instrument. There was the friendly honk, the nudge that signified his presence and the outright blare. He conducted a deft symphony of the three as he edged us through the traffic. With cars from three roads merging onto ours the honks in the air became a strange orchestra. Beyond the beads hanging in the front window I saw women in shawls having their hands hennaed under awnings. Behind me, the two Chinese women the driver had also picked up sat hunched, silent. My attempts to engage the driver in conversation, using pidgin French, had just encouraged him to sell me a tour of the city. 'Non,' I insisted, pointing to the phone on my map. 'La Terrasse des Espices.'

He looked bored rather than irritated – as if the attempt to sell to me was a formality. When we arrived I pressed the 60 Dirham into his hands at the entrance to the souk.

My phone buzzed in my pocket as I got out. Maria.

They are throwing the cases against Velasco out unless some evidence comes out in the next few days.

The text infuriated me. Here I was, on another continent, working for that very cause. What was *she* doing? I had gone to the court, accepting the tacit accusation I was playing the role of a white knight. What more could I do? But despite my anger the thought of Velasco being exonerated frayed my nerves.

I replied:

No pressure then.

And then, I thought about the stinging feeling the world left me in, and what it suggested, as I typed:

Sounds to me like they've already made up their mind. And that they're saying that to look open-minded but in fact he got off.

I pushed the phone into my pocket and wiped my brow, glad that the interior of the souk was cool. Boys in mopeds forced me to press against the walls as they darted down the alleyways. The souk seemed to narrow as I followed the thin blue line on Google Maps. Each time I glanced at a row of hanging brass lamps, a series of paintings or a display of ceramics a smiling vendor asked me where I was from, if I would like to take a look, where was I going? A bulging sense of stress joined with the pulsing pain just under my heart. It was ever present, like a half-forgotten insult. I decided that thoughts of Francine were an indulgence I could not afford right now. I just focused on going down the tunnel. A series of hanging signs with vague arrows took me down a smaller souk, and up a series of steps.

On the first floor tourists sat on barrels, sipped Mojitos and tucked into terrines. Carrots constructed in a pyre over a hunk of boned chicken. A vendor pointed me to the terrace, up a tiny flight of steps. With each step the humidity grew stronger. How would I recognise Rosalie when I saw her?

I reminded myself of the mental gap between fantasy and reality. In my mind I expected Rosalie to be a chic woman in a light summer dress, an elegant shawl around her head. I recalibrated myself, knowing that my image was unrealistic. That was not how life worked – one bad event preceded another.

I knew that I needed to sink to the bottom of this state of mind before any upswing would take place. I decided Rosalie would be late, sweaty, or even absent. The days of Maria and Francine jostling for my attention were gone; that bubble had burst. I'd been fortunate it had ever floated.

The stairway bloomed open like a ceramic flower, its edges decorated with black and white pictures of celebrities. Nicholas Cage grinned at me from behind a thin façade of dirt. I looked around the terrace. The Marrakech sky, rising from white to deep blue around the edge of the skyline, was a rich spectacle. The air was soothing and laced with spaces. In each corner of the terrace people ate on high tables, or cowered from the late afternoon sun under canopies.

A maître d' in a chequered shirt blocked me with an artfully placed menu. 'No food for one person,' he said.

'I'm meeting someone,' I answered, as I looked past him. I could see a woman sat on the other side of the roof garden, in a booth. Her slenderness and long, blonde hair suggested a kind of mournful serenity. The centre parting and the pout of her lips only enhanced it. She seemed engaged with something on her lap. 'Rosalie,' I said – more for him than for her. He pushed me over to her with a smile.

Her invisible shroud shifted as she looked up at me.

'I'm Jude,' I said.

'Oh. I expected you to look different, somehow,' she said with a slight smile.

Her English was poised, with only a slight hint of Spanish apparent around the vowels. It suggested a well-travelled youth, and the type of cosmopolitan persona Francine had tended to resent.

Somehow chastened, I sat on the cushioned bench opposite her. A silver pot of Arabic tea sat beside her, an ornate glass filled with yellow liquid. She offered some, and I accepted with a nod. For a Spaniard in Marrakech her blonde paleness surprised me. I recalled Maria mentioning her studying in Paris between stays in Morocco. In her words Rosalie had recently 'been struggling'. I wondered how much these difficulties related to her grandfather. If so, how easy would it be to get to his diaries?

As I settled, sunlight caught the side of her hair. Her dress was white, and for a moment it reminded me of a cassock. It undermined the air of saintly, martyrish pain that she somehow exuded. As she poured the tea she did so with the air of someone re-enacting an ancient Japanese ceremony. She smiled at me and I decided that my attraction to her was on principle. Then I reminded myself this was the granddaughter of Velasco.

'Thank you,' I said. 'I'm parched.'

I wondered if I would tell her of my encounter with her grandfather. But as I followed her shaking hand she looked as if she might shatter at a moment's notice.

15

Some mental tussle, evident for a second in her glowering expression, was soon vented. 'I should make something clear straight away,' she said, suspending her cup between two hands like a chalice. 'I have disowned my grandfather. Do you have any idea what it's like to be descended from a man who hurt so many people?'

I noticed that her Spanish accent grew stronger with anger. I sipped the tea, finding it sickly-sweet. I imagined a life in which I would become accustomed to its tang. I shook my head.

She shuddered. 'It feels dreadful to have something so ... *méchant,* so nasty, in your blood.'

I wondered what it would be like to flit between languages as you articulated yourself. What worlds of expression were opened up by the ability?

'I can only imagine. I must admit, your grandfather has taken up a lot of space in my head.'

'What do you mean?' she asked, narrowing her eyes.

'I'm talking about the miscarriage of justice.'

'You are assuming he is guilty?'

'I met his victims.' My tone was colder than I had intended it to be.

'My family is divided over this. I think he escaped justice,' she said. 'But my father thinks he was set up. I have watched him give interviews to the newspapers, calling these women money grabbers and liars.' She held her temple between her thumb and forefinger. 'I just don't know what to think.'

'So how do you feel about sharing his diaries with me?'

She pressed her fingers against her temple. 'One step at a time, Jude,' she said.

I felt my anger rise, hot and acrid in my throat. How could she hesitate? Someone had come to help her face the truth and yet still she was reluctant. But then that word *méchant* echoed in my mind. She wanted the truth. Yet perhaps she didn't want it confirmed that she was descended from a monster. A monster that her father was still defending. It was her conviction that she feared the most. I could not help wondering where that conviction came from. Looking at her, rubbing her temple, I felt a rush of sympathy.

'Fair enough,' I said. I was reminded of Maria's distress, when we had first met. Those expressions of hers, bridling with conflict and assertion. Rosalie's expressions were composed from a different palette; I could only guess at its colours.

'There's one question I must ask,' I said. 'What do you think happened to Valdez?'

She looked like she might snap at me, but then she leant back. The hair around her centre parting fell, hard as a curtain. 'I don't know what really went on between the two of them. I sometimes think of my grandfather's diaries *simmering* away in Casablanca. He had his holiday home there. It was the place where he got away from it all. If he confessed during his lifetime, it will be in those books. I used to walk in as a little girl and he would always be writing. I had assumed he was doing academic work, but now I think he was laying himself out in those pages.'

'Yet something has stopped you opening them.'

'This has all happened so soon,' she whispered.

'To be frank with you, I am here to see what he put in those pages. I'm also desperate to see Valdez's archives. I am hoping they'll reveal what exactly happened to him.'

I remembered my dreams about unending sheaves of paper. They had begun the moment I had been told to finish Valdez's collection and they hadn't let up since. In those dreams blizzards of pages swarmed around me, thickening until I struggled to breathe. Within the fragile boundaries of the dream, I somehow knew one page would solve the mystery about Valdez. But as I tried to grab them they melted like snow in my hands. I would catch one and see a few words before they vanished. Amongst the thick texture of the dream it was impossible to remember even those words. Like snowflakes, they contained whole universes, and melted at the human touch.

She nodded at me, her eyes trembling. 'Maybe you can help me face up to it all. Maybe you are brave enough to go there.'

'I don't know about that. What I am is ... angry and confused.'

I'm also someone running away from the absurd questions in his own life, I thought.

'Confused? What confuses *you*?' she asked.

I took a deep breath. 'Why an artist of such great sensitivity would become so close to ... your grandfather.'

Heat and hunger had eroded my sensitivity. I expected her to bite back at me. But she clicked her fingers, and her eyes sharpened. 'That – right there – is the question I can't answer. I see why my grandfather wanted to get close to Valdez. But why the other why round?'

She leant forward.

'I suspect Valdez wanted to be close to my grandfather,' she said, 'because he saw what a monster he was. I think he wanted to keep the monster close, to remind him—'

'Of what he could be.'

Her smile suggested I had passed some invisible exam.

'We'll get the next train to Casa,' she said. 'You can dive into both of the archives.' She placed her hands behind her head. 'Perhaps you can be the one to confirm how tainted my blood is.'

I laughed. 'I can do that,' I said. As if it was no great issue to me.

'Okay,' she answered. Her tone had brightened. It was as if the shroud had been pulled away. 'But first, we should eat.'

She looked over my shoulders. 'We should take in the Marrakech sunset. Then we can go into – what did Conrad call it? '*The Heart of Darkness*'.'

It was a hollow, bookish joke, but it gave me a sense of dread.

16

Any hope that the journey from Marrakech would reveal Rosalie's secrets was soon dashed.

A long queue in a sweltering station revealed that first-class seats were sold out. Rosalie translated the verdict of the woman behind the glass with bitterness. We would need to fight it out for a seat or for somewhere to stand, she said.

I responded to the news with what I hoped was a spirited attitude, refreshing my rucksack on my shoulder. But Rosalie's brow was creased. Once our tickets had been checked on the platform I could see why.

We pushed down the narrow corridors of the train, trying to find a seat. We passed sealed compartments crammed with people, illuminated only by flickering overhead lights. In the carriages men glowered up at us, and with brusque gestures blocked vacant seats with their bags. We pushed down further. I again felt like I was entering a tunnel. With each step the train grew hotter. 'How long is the journey?' I asked.

'Three hours,' she said, as we surged into the next carriage.

This one was even fuller, and the thick miasma that enclosed us confirmed the air conditioning was broken.

We leant between two package cases at the end of the carriage – the only space to stand. I realised that attempts to kindle a conversation in these conditions would be futile and I preoccupied myself with my map. 'Did you know this journey goes right through the desert?' I asked, trying to distract myself from the humidity.

She blew the fringe from her forehead. It was slick with sweat. 'Yeah. We're going through the desert, in the dark,' she said.

I thought of her Conrad quote. I felt like I was going up the river to find Colonel Kurtz, a man driven mad by an ego that took him into exile. This seemed like a one-way mission to find a vanished man.

'But you've done this before?' I asked.

'From Marrakech? Only first thing in the morning.' She peered at a woman in a heavy burka, wiping the steam from the window with her sleeve. 'That is one of the most beautiful trips you can make,' she said. 'I used to do it when I visited my grandmother.'

'Your grandfather too?' I asked.

The train jolted to life.

She grabbed an overhead strap. 'Yeah, him too,' she said.

Her lips curled at me for a moment. The pristine, pale woman I had met on the terrace was transforming as we moved towards Casablanca.

The train shunted from the station. The overhead lights blinked off and then on as it moved.

I switched between checking my phone and tracing the journey on the map. Rosalie's silence seemed determined. The palm trees, just visible through the dirty windows, began to become scarcer as the train roared along the track. As the night grew darker the palm trees faded into the gloom.

'We must be in the desert,' she said, looking over my shoulder.

Almost as if on cue, the momentum of the train faltered, the roar of its movement fading. The train began to slow. The lights winked out. Rosalie grasped my elbow. 'What's happening?' she asked.

A wail of frustration rose from the silhouetted heads and shoulders in the carriage. The train stopped with a sickening clunk. A moment later iPhones flickered to life. Some activated the flashlights on their mobiles. They flickered like fireflies in the hot darkness. When I took out my phone, Rosalie snapped at me.

'You should turn it off. If the train can't move we might need it,' she said.

16

I looked at the screen. There was a single message from Maria:

We have two days to get evidence or Velasco's victims get nothing.

I turned my phone off and closed my eyes. The legalistic proforma the world operated in; completely out of synch with the slow, gradual movement across emotional material required to really address an issue. But then in turn, the degree to which developments moving at a glacial pace often smacked of corruption.

As I stood in the stifling darkness, I thought that from somewhere in the desert I could hear Velasco laughing at me. The air grew hotter.

Throughout the carriage arguments broke out in bitter Arabic. Babies started crying, and urgent words from their mothers didn't quiet them. This further enraged the men, who started to berate them.

I pressed against the air conditioning rail. I could see no way to open the windows above us. Screams went up. A woman at the other end of the carriage had fainted. I had dismissed the dull thump of her body as an outside noise. But now, the black curve of her burqa was ominous in its stasis. When one woman tried to make her way past us to the toilet, she assumed Rosalie was blocking her. 'Naql,' she urged. Men looked at us with narrowed eyes. I imagined Rosalie and I as two sun-stroked blots, cowering. The shame added to the claustrophobia and fear, our discomfort layering.

I found myself closing my eyes, trying to imagine comforting moments from my childhood. But I couldn't concentrate. The heat was too overpowering. I couldn't move amongst the sweating bodies. All I could do, moment to moment, was hope that the train started moving or that someone opened the doors.

I thought of the desert, cool and wide. I wanted nothing more than a clean, empty room where I could cool my skin. When accepting the award I had never thought I would end up in this position. Why was I here? What decisions had taken me to this point?

It occurred to me how often, during my youth, I had fallen into self-pity. If I didn't have enough money for a decent meal, or if I hadn't heard from a woman I fancied; if my flat was damp or my work was insecure. But in those moments I had never considered what I did have. I had never had to experience a single night outdoors. I had never had to experience discomfort without an end in sight. I had been ill-prepared for the future ahead of me, one that had no obligation to cater for me. Was this journey preparing me for what lay ahead?

I inhaled a lungful of stale, hot air. My head felt as if it was going to split open. I had a dark thought. Perhaps at the end of this there would not be a revelation. Perhaps Velasco would remain unknowable; a black box. Perhaps this discomfort was just that: discomfort. It was not a penance, nor a preparation. It was the onslaught of some reality that I had been too cosseted to appreciate before now.

A shiver circled around my heart. This was my punishment for seeking answers I did not deserve.

But I now had more immediate concerns.

I checked my belongings, emboldened by a sense of panic. I had a warm bottle of water, a tube of cleaning fluid, a half-eaten sandwich, and a map. Through the gloom I saw Rosalie conduct her own private inventory. Having made her verdict, she shook her head in despair. To stave off a sense of panic I offered her some water. As she took a pensive sip my heart slowed. I realised I was able to endure far more than I had appreciated. Every time I told myself 'this is my limit', and that I was about to pass out, there were whole new levels of endurance I was surprised to find.

I tried to steady myself on my feet. Something about the situation made me want to laugh. I was learning about myself; perhaps that was good?

A door behind us burst open and cooler air trickled into the compartment. The relief amongst the hunched bodies was palpable. From outside, the shout *'akhraj'* went up. 'Get out,' Rosalie echoed.

The silhouettes padded themselves as they assembled in the desert. The night air was so cold it was painful. It blasted over the hot sweat on my skin, making me dizzy. I could feel sweat on my back even though I was freezing.

The way some people checked their bags suggested we were out here for the night. It was a suspicion confirmed by the grey smoke spewing from the engine at the front of the train. I wondered if a gasket was blown. I saw the conductor arguing with the driver, who threw his hands in the air and walked away. His head and shoulders were illuminated as he stopped and held his phone aloft.

With each passing moment the cold clasped around us. Lights were visible in the distance. I suspected they were not electric. 'Some people live out in the desert,' Rosalie whispered.

I resolved to be positive; for her sake as well as mine. To my surprise with this determination I felt the negativity in my mind being doused, and replaced with something cleansing. Despite my surroundings I realised that the contents of my mind remained mine and mine alone. Whatever happened, I got to choose them. I made a mental note of the realisation, knowing I would need it.

As women shared their concerns from behind burkas their breath formed silver clouds in front of them. The men argued with each other and remonstrated with the driver. Rosalie turned to me and patted herself. 'I am starting to think this journey might have been a mistake,' she said.

17

Rosalie leant against the doorframe in the office, her eyes following me as I passed her and took a seat at the desk. As I settled down I took in that expansive green garden, rolling down to a grey-blue ocean. I took a deep breath.

Arriving at the house the night before I had been too relieved to consider the glacial beauty of the place. The trip had taken me to such an extreme mental state that my longing for a bath and a sleep had been my only concerns. Four hours in the freezing desert waiting for a repairs truck and another two and a half on that hot box of a train. Something told me that discomfort had created in me a state of mind necessary for the challenge ahead. I had been given the tools I needed the moment before I was required to use them. I knew this did not bode well for the contents of the archive.

'It's all here?' I asked, turning to the twelve boxes on the desk. Some were huge removal cardboard boxes, others mere shoeboxes.

Her shadow fell over me. 'He's all there,' she said. 'He's all yours, now.'

That morning I had been surprised by the heft of the boxes. As I'd shifted them, one by one, from the attic to the desk they had felt as heavy as breezeblocks. They were as unwieldy, as undignified as a heavy corpse. It had felt perverse and invasive to move them.

Rosalie, lightly directing me from the bottom of the stairs, had been happy to let me sweat over the struggle. As I'd tried to find a surface for the final box the bottom of it had split. Papers of all hues had spilt through my hands. It occurred to me at that moment, covered in him, that these papers were not meant to be kept, moved, or considered. They were part of Valdez's artistic bloodstream. Who was I to get immersed in all this?

Rosalie's phrase, 'He's all there,' reverberated as I turned to the first box. When I had first sat at that desk, amongst the statuettes and abstract prints of the office, the house had held an exotic air. But now the air was heavy with responsibility.

Was there enough in this archive to shed light on where Valdez went? I was conscious that in an upstairs office there was a smaller bundle of Velasco's diaries waiting for me. I suspected they contained the real poison that I was hoping to draw out here. Maria's insistent texts did not alter the fact that I was not ready for that task. Valdez's unanswered questions would come first. I felt as if I was following a process. First of all I had to take on the lesser challenge. To ascend the foothills of insight, before I could reach any pinnacle. Despite no one having tutored me about the unseen process ahead, I seemed at some point to have tapped into a collective knowledge. It was a sensation that was unfamiliar.

In the bright afternoon sun the piles of boxes looked like pieces of a monumental puzzle. Pulling up a chair beside me Rosalie commented on how much easier it had been when he had been 'a tight lattice in the attic'. I preferred the phrase 'walled off annex', but kept that to myself. I was the surveyor of the rotting cellar, the pathologist at the crime scene. Meanwhile, she was contenting herself with the role of someone who'd 'happened' to find the body. She was merely waiting for the post-mortem.

It wasn't the moving of the pieces that had disturbed me, it was the thought of creating a composite whole out of them. How could you begin to assemble the puzzle that is a person? Rosalie was mistaken. He was not 'all here'. He was somewhere – but it wasn't here. However heavy these pieces were they still wouldn't create a complete picture of him. The journey here had taught me that strain was not proof of success. Strain could be improving, but of itself it wasn't a destination. Pieces of the puzzle were missing; and the more I looked for them the more glaring their absence became. But how did I know they were missing if I did not know what the pieces were?

The spilt box seemed the least indecent place to start. I let it spill onto the floor. Rosalie let out a hollow laugh and folded her arms.

There was such a sense of haphazardness about the multi-coloured documents that it was clear Rosalie had not ordered the contents. The way she leant over them, fingers touching her throat, betrayed her queasiness. Ideas must have spilt from Valdez at every moment. He must have worked in such a state of intellectual fury that he could not direct the stream of his output. Was this all a person was – a fountain of ideas? With these documents the drying droplets?

I charted the content of each box in a notebook. If my annex metaphor had been the accurate metaphor I was now walking through the architecture of his mind.

One shoebox was full of juvenilia. There was a shoebox full of early writings – fragments of stories and some hastily written novellas. They grasped my attention for a few hours. Rosalie flittered in and out like a ghost. These fragments were written in English – Valdez's long practised method to ensure no one else could read his work. I wondered if the coincidence was too pat, and then remembered that I had first been drawn to him for his love of the English language. This early writing was lucid to the point of being hallucinatory – a sensual Spanish childhood rendered in precise English prose. He described live music with raw, synesthetic language. He recounted afternoons spent on beaches swimming in the ocean, as if they were quasi-religious experiences.

The next few shoeboxes were correspondences. Letters from women he'd dated – or almost dated. There were many disparate threads to his private life here, shimmering and neglected, spiders' webs lit by morning dew, unlamented when ripped out by a gentle breeze. If they intrigued me then these unconsummated relationships must have tormented him. If this was the aggregate of his life then what did we make of these loose ends? How relevant were they? I thought of the unborn children, the divorces terminated before they had become necessary. Amongst this debris time was reflexive; possibilities were splayed open and left in that state, with their originator absent, unable to follow them. I was amongst the sticky web of his life and couldn't help envying the possibilities that had been open to him. Had he been assigned talents that placed him in a superior order?

Rosalie read these correspondences to me. The prose varied in ferocity, depending on how intimately he'd been involved with the woman. She read them in halting, whispered words, as if soothing the heat that rose from those pages. Some showed him pleading for reunions; others described romantic set pieces with precision. He'd coaxed something out of these women that they had struggled to put back into the box after his departure. He picked through the remains of these affairs with the salaciousness of a desperate man. I got the sense of him remaining in control even when portraying himself as in a state of abandon. These sequences were in themselves a controlled performance. He tried out guises and masks, and saw which disintegrated themselves. Somewhere amongst these false starts would emerge the Valdez I got to know, but he was a negotiation, a remainder.

There was a box of finished and unfinished short stories, written in English. Only in certain passages did a freshness and a boldness that I associated with Valdez ooze out. Despite the naivety of these stories they coaxed tears from my eyes. As I read them, the room rang with laughter. Rosalie would appear in the doorway to ask what I'd found. I would read out sections and she sipped tea as I became a ventriloquist for

Valdez. I played to her reactions, once or twice I even riffed on what he was saying as I enjoyed the sound of laugher, pretending it was his words I was speaking. Valdez was lost in translation again.

It occurred to me that we were taking it in turns to perform as a dead man. It also felt as if we were bringing him back to life, revelling in his company. It was strange to have him in the room; it was almost a distillation of the surreal nature of his work. We had no right to interpret him in this way, his absence both ensured that and demanded it too.

There were numbers for utility companies that he needed to call. Reminders of letters to be sent. Each Peseta he spent was accounted for. I surmised that he must've been poor and it made me understand him more.

There were one or two diaries, which I found myself savouring and jealously guarding from Rosalie. I was inside his interior at last.

The diaries described him moving to a new city. As he'd immersed himself in the artistic scene he'd written invigorating reflections. I got a sense of a man trying out different personas; the surreal and impulsive persona the public came to know him for must have been found at this time. There were early press cuttings, torn out of respective publications and placed between pages. There were diary entries in which he described chatting up the women on the cosmetics desks of a local department store. He made notes of chat-up lines that worked. He wasn't just crafting linguistic trophies here. He was annotating when his intuitions and bold strategies had paid off.

It occurred to me that a person of high achievement was likely to undertake such efficiencies, and be keen to push boundaries. They did not want to repeat donkeywork and mundane tasks like most humans. Their eventual notoriety and resonance was not a mistake; it had been crafted from the sticky, burning tar of existence.

I wondered if this was a man who collected women as some collect butterflies. Not just to trap or exploit them but to try and keep himself in a state of perpetual awe, itself an obtuse and selfish assignation. In the diaries there would be long ruminations about the backgrounds of women he'd met in passing. It was hard to know where fiction and fact ended. Sometimes his fiction seemed a catharsis, a way to will into existence a certain relationship or lifestyle through the intensity offered by sustained attention. It seemed undeniable to me; the narrative you placed someone in had its own unique power glowing from it. Move yourself closer to it and become invested in it; neglect it and it feeds.

I could see why Rosalie felt intoxicated by the idea he was somewhere in this web. The web had so many facets, so many strands. Some were sticky and problematic, some were under-formed, some glistened when held up to the light. Just as I was unable to step far enough back from the boxes in this small room to see them all at once so too was I unable to step far enough back to get a sense of the whole man. There was no guarantee that the archive would reveal where he went. Puzzle pieces did not promise a complete picture. Yet I told myself that the answer had to be in there somewhere.

It was with a shudder of relief that I found his later diaries. His sloping handwriting was more condensed by then, as if the sheer stress of life had compressed his words. These notes were tidier; they revealed to me that Valdez knew time was running out. Perhaps on some intuitive level he had long known that, and it had inspired the intensity of his work.

After an almost fifteen-year gap these diaries began mid-sentence. He mentioned his fiftieth birthday party and the existential crisis that began these notes. The diaries ended weeks before his death, as a quick ordering of them on the desk proved. Flicking through the notebooks, I saw how some of the writing had been ferocious enough to pierce the page. The thought of someone's expressions tearing their chosen medium excited me; I was close to the white-hot heat of existence. I realised that if there were answers they would be here. If there was a secret medical or psychological condition then this was the place.

But to my surprise, these diaries focused mainly on flirtations he'd had at the various universities he visited. As I read them with increased intensity – aware of the blue darkness outside the window – I felt the dark chilling of my blood. What if I was about to learn how similar he was to Velasco? Brief mentions of his friend's charitable assistance were the only links I had seen between the two of them.

'What is it?' Rosalie asked.

I turned to see her holding two cups of coffee.

'His first mentions of Velasco. They're few and far between.'

'Do they talk about … his women?'

I found it an unpleasant choice of phrase. Them not being *his* had been the whole point, but I knew she knew that. I thought of Maria. What would she think of these indulgent speculations, when a more pressing truth awaited upstairs? I tried to push the thought away, but it lingered.

She placed two mugs on the table. 'Can I suggest you don't torture yourself any longer? Read his final diaries and work out if he really killed himself. Then *go upstairs*. Read Velasco's diaries.' She swept her hand over the boxes. 'The rest can wait.'

I nodded. 'Okay,' I said.

I went upstairs, and peered in at Velasco's office. I looked at the neat pile of diaries. When I remembered how Velasco had made me feel the idea of entering his mental interior was disgusting. Unlike Valdez's interior, which had been sensual, surreal and erotic I was sure Velasco's would contain the mundaneness of the self-indulgent. I reminded myself there were more important issues at stake. I went into my bedroom opposite the study, and turned on my phone. I felt very alone with my thoughts, and with the slow heave of my body as I waited. A message from Maria flashed up.

If there is no evidence out there, just admit it. No one will blame you. But either way we really need to know. TONIGHT.

I looked back at Velasco's pile. Its stasis mocked me. I walked downstairs, and told myself I would return in a few hours.

18

In Valdez's final diaries there was a gradual but pronounced shift. During the era following his divorce he moved into a flat – paid for by the university – on the outskirts of Barcelona. Here, he begins to unravel fast. The fluid, energetic prose becomes fractured. His words are a series of images, placed next to one another with seeming precision and yet without clear linkages.

One short story that gripped me was about a ballerina who fantasised about losing her limbs. I wondered if Valdez's mind – freed at this point by not having to worry about money – now had *too* much time to flex itself. His mental dexterity started to take in all possibilities, and consider all philosophical options. As a ballerina might fantasise about injury saving her from the pains of perfection, he fantasised about not being able to strive for truth, about his God given ability being blunted and excusing himself from a difficult game.

I flickered through the pages faster and faster. Towards the end of his life he too was expressing himself faster and faster. There was a ravishing adeptness about the way he veered from being inside the mind of a damaged dancer to being inside the mind of a gored matador. It wasn't that one of those characters revealed his essence, it was that both did; they all did. Even those fragments gave way to darker ones. Quotes from Van Gogh and Pyrrho of Elis, where the only prevailing theme was doubt. Valdez reflected on Freud's death drive, and pasted around those riffs are photos of films stars that died young. Frances Farmer, James Dean, Gene Tierney. The man himself was floating amongst these aesthetic compass points. That collage suggested he was presenting, to himself the glamour of an early death. I had the sensation of an invisible white heat rising off these pages. The incantatory glow of a person crafting their meaning to its finest mortal point, leaving fragments of insight in their wake. This is it, I thought. These are the *real* pieces of the puzzle that together will explain his vanishing.

As the writing became less and less coherent the dates tallied with him being checked in to a local hospital. Rave notices from his last novel were stuck alongside facsimiles of huge hospital bills. Here Valdez was presenting the twin peaks of his life to himself, by visually juxtaposing the two.

Ferocious exchanges with a psychiatrist sit alongside unsent letters to his book designer. He speculates on the value of absenting yourself from normal life. He ponders the lessons of Nietzsche, who he says proposed such a strategy. He debates the value of Marlon Brando's late worldview. The moment he has boiled this thesis down to a single sentence he abandons it. He ravages religious texts like a frenzied accountant making his way through a pile of tax returns. Here, Valdez's intellect is working faster than his empathy, and his cynicism calcifies. It is almost as if he has mastered the great philosophies and found them all wanting.

He has plundered the work of the great poets, thinkers and actors. Having squeezed them of their value he moves on. He's exhumed the insights of human kind and now, alone on his quest, he is stepping beyond them. It felt utterly thrilling to be alongside him; to be the first to be so. As he tests the capacity of language to reveal truth a kind of supernatural thread seems to float between his words. He moves between English, Spanish, French and Greek – can anyone follow him now? A revelation floats above the pages, unseen and not manifested. It becomes clear to me that humankind uses compassion and art to cultivate a sense of meaning, to connect with something greater. We are all limited by our faulty antennae, which at best flicker in and out of their connection with the transcendent. Here Valdez is in the realm of Newton, Einstein and Da Vinci; he's the finger between him and God. How do I know there is a transcendent? I feel it in the work of those standing tallest, and in how they strain to reach it.

Yet his day-to-day life roots him in the reality of ward rounds and scheduled dinners. He addresses the mundane with the morbid curiosity of a man who has seen the greatest sunsets. His diaries become full of sketched encounters with fellow patients in the hospital, but I sense that in this widening gulf madness is burgeoning. One extended riff, about a Greek journalist he befriends on the ward, contains some of his most lucid writing in years. During group therapy sessions she is the only person he has any time for. He describes how 'her natural darkness lifts at a moment's notice', and how this reminds him of 'the possibility of relief (transcendence)'. He describes their conversations over cigarettes in the hospital garden. She relays the struggles of trying to expose corruption at a local newspaper. Velasco is mentioned, in teasing references to 'my troubled friend'. I wonder whether Valdez knew of his friend's behaviour at this point, and if he condemned it. Both of them are preoccupied with the pursuit of women, and I wonder if they ever negotiated their divergent approaches on this. One line snags my attention: 'Velasco has started an affair with one of his followers. I think flattery played a large role.'

I found myself reading the line again and again and I thought of Lily; not a student, someone who I had a position of power over. Was this the start of Velasco's moral slide? Had that potentially been the start of mine? I had glimpsed what taking that fork in the road had felt like, without even taking it. It had felt like a painful, unremitting route which at some point I'd been expected to continue to travel on my own.

The thought sent me into a panic. Every ghost seemed to have broken out, wild and whirling. But, for some reason, the wait in the desert had steeled my resolve. I pushed on.

There is then a gap of a few months. During this time Valdez was supposed to have his first literary tour, but it was cancelled as a result of ill health. I was frustrated to see no more writing about his best friend, but at this point he has bigger issues to contend with. His accelerating brain is starting to exhaust his body, and daily boredom compounds the problem. His pasted psychiatric reports are the only insights into him that he offers at this point. They are placed onto the pages with the defiance of someone who has lost faith in their own articulacy. It now feels as if he is beyond the mortal realm.

Rosalie read these reports out, and as she did so her lilting tone became deeper. Even the psychiatrist seems reluctant to set down, in black and white, Valdez's mental state. Valdez has apparently been telling him about the Iranian writer Sadegh Hedayat, whose book *The Blind Owl* was said to offer such devastating insights into the human condition that it provoked mass suicides. Valdez is quoted as saying: 'If I was to write a book of what I have seen, it would obliterate mankind.' The psychiatrist recounts him boasting of an ability to read the layers of a human being just by meeting them. Valdez states that he knows, in intricate detail, the fate of mankind. He is quoted as saying: 'I have enough evidence to know this is not madness, but accelerated insight.' These reports suggest that these sessions became a verbal jousting match. The psychiatrist writes: 'He finds even my company limited. Valdez's readiness to switch between philosophical, spiritual and scientific language recall the late ramblings of electricity pioneer Nikola Tesla.'

That night I read until I slumped asleep on the desk, my head in my hands. Rosalie woke me up. I felt as if I hadn't slept; it had been a few hours at most. My eyes stung – they felt raw and exposed. I thought of Valdez's words smouldering away in there, like a shallow fire. As I pulled on my clothes my head was still full of dreams in which Velasco taunted me. The differences between the two men, and their unsaid conversations, were being negotiated somewhere at the back of my brain. I emerged from the box room exhausted.

I made my way down the stairs, my eyes adjusting to the light filtering in from outside. I took a deep breath as I sat down opposite Rosalie on the terrace. A brutal and energetic sea was battering the shore, and the infusion of salt in the air made my red eyes sting. As she sipped coffee I wondered if the calm expression on her face was a mask. Her heavy blue gown looked a touch Victorian and gave the breakfast something of a colonial air.

As we ate toast I could see, on a patch of beach, dark-skinned men playing football. Wives and girlfriends looked on from under hijabs, immobile on their deckchairs. As she poured us tea I roused myself to speak. I asked her why Velasco had chosen this location for his holiday home. Any conversation that kept me away from written words for a few moments longer now seemed a blessing.

'Casablanca was an odd choice for my grandfather,' she said, casting an eye over me. I became conscious of my crumpled appearance. 'My grandfather once said he wanted to live in a country poorer than Spain, so he would feel rich.' She sipped her drink. 'I suspect that in his diaries he'll give us the reason,' she said.

I bridled at the weak attempt to motivate me. Was she using me as a pioneer into darkness she couldn't experience?

I sipped the coffee, and felt the tension ease around my jaw. I had not been aware of it until it eased a little. I had never known my mind race with such urgency. These pulsating days had the intensity of adolescent love affairs. They had the potency of events that will reverberate for the rest of your life. Something told me that when the tally of my life would be added up the next few hours would be key. I was conflicted; on the one hand the train journey here had prepared me for this intensity, on the other hand that trip had exhausted me before I had even begun.

What plan did destiny have for me, and how precisely was it unfurling?

It was almost as if I had one foot in another place, in the land of the dead. I considered whether in moments of significance we are closer to the dead than ever. I wondered then if destiny sent us guides for portions of our journey. Where we delivered ferrymen to guide us through the darker realms? I told myself not to give in to such reflections, and the discipline with which my mind obeyed suggested it had been strengthened.

I looked up at Rosalie. As she smiled at me I felt an extra-human, wordless connection with her.

Her expression suggested she was contending with a very different thought. 'You know, my grandfather was a big Humphrey Bogart fan,' she said. 'Perhaps that is all there was to it.' She leant forward. 'Do you ever worry that all this symbolism is just ... confusing?'

'Sure. In the absence of evidence it does get to the point where symbolism and belief offer the only answers.' I looked up at her with a smile I intended to be stoical. 'It's not a very satisfying thought, I admit,' I said.

'So what are you hoping to find in my grandfather's diaries?'

'I have two more volumes of Valdez to get through first.'

She exhaled.

'What is it?' I asked.

Her eyes focused on the cup in front of her. 'Look, I know it should be me who's opening my grandfather's diaries. But it's understandable that I am reluctant.'

'What are you saying?'

She looked out at the sea. 'I don't know. When I was a little girl...' she looked at me. 'It's hard to describe. Your memories get vague. When you try to capture them they become like a photocopy of a photocopy.'

'Are you saying that he...'

She didn't want to hear the end of my sentence. 'I don't know if he did anything to me. But what I do know is that I believe the women.'

'I do too.'

'Yes,' she said, eyes burning. 'But it's not about you. Despite what may or may not have happened I really resent having a man come in here, playing the role of a white knight.'

Her eyes narrowed on the women in the hijabs. I waited for the sting of her remark to subside. It didn't.

'The diaries are up there. You could open them yourself.'

She looked at me, her lip curling. 'You met these women, Jude. You looked them in the eye. Yet you're only getting round to looking at the evidence – even though it's time sensitive – when it suits you.'

I was shocked to see the teacups shaking. Her voice had grown louder without me realising. The sudden rousing of the birds behind me confirmed it.

'I'm scared of what I'm going to find too. That train ride toughened me up a bit, but I have no idea —'

She interrupted me. 'Jude, it's just not about you.'

I looked past her. 'I know that.'

'Look, Jude, I'm sorry. I know you're trying to help. I know it's not as if I'm facing up to the facts either, but I'm doing a damn sight better than most of my family. But helping these women ... it's not a part-time job.'

'I will look. Today. But what if it's...'

'What?'

'I don't know!' I felt my patience unspool. 'It could be vivid descriptions of rape for all I know!'

'For Christ's sake. Hundreds of thousands of rapists all over the world. Millions of men fantasising about rape, looking up rape on the Internet. And I get the one bleeding heart scared to take any ownership of his sex.'

'I'm scared to take ownership? Well, if it's so tame why don't you look?' I put my head in my hands.

I was jolted as she slammed her hands on the table. 'Because for all I know I'm in those pages, Jude! Something about my past; something that I have tried very hard to forget!'

I knew I was too sleepy to appreciate that she had just revealed the key to her conflict. 'Just because it didn't happen to me, doesn't mean I'm not scared of it,' I said.

'Oh, spare me,' she hissed. 'Face it, Jude. You're scared of yourself. You're a man, and you're scared of whether you're any different to him. A pretty girl comes onto you, heaven forbid with a little persistence and tenacity – who knows for what reasons – and all these principles you wring your hands over get lost. What a luxury to worry about such things! You know what women are scared of, Jude? Getting raped. You're scared of what ambiguous situations you might have got into and what that makes you. You're scared that one day if you have any success you'll be just as bad as he was.'

I waited until the words had faded. I knew they were for me, but that in another way they were for him. But they seemed to seep into my skin. She focused on me as I tried to think of a response. But, remembering Lily, I realised I just didn't have one. She was right.

'What is it, Jude? You might as well say it after everything else we've said.'

I looked at her. 'I suppose you're right,' I said.

Her lip curl didn't fade. 'See? It isn't so hard to face up to the truth. When you open his diaries brace yourself for the nature of reality. There may be vague clues, but nothing definitive,' she said, her tone level.

'Okay. Why do you say that?'

'People don't know what they're doing, they're in flux.' She looked out at the sea. 'And here's you poring through it all, looking for definitive answers.'

'I'm looking for evidence. Not just to help me, but to help the victims.'

'If you really cared you'd have gone to my grandfather's diaries first,' she said, looking at her hands. 'And they're not victims, they're women, with whole other lives. Ambitions. Inner worlds. They didn't plan to get labelled as victims when they were starting their lives out. And I hear a decision is about to be made about their lives very soon.'

I looked around myself, unable to refute the accusations. 'I wonder if this house will be sold?'

She bit her lip. 'I don't give a damn if it is. My grandfather treated people in an ugly way. And this place is beautiful. In a weird way selling this place to give the victims money might offer some balance.' She looked around herself. 'Not that it can fix anything.'

I realised how badly I wanted to see, in Velasco's diaries, proof of mental torment. A torment worse than any Valdez had experienced. It was ironic that the great artist had suffered, and the man who had exploited the art had not. I wanted evidence that there was a price for his crimes.

But there was Valdez's work to finish.

I raced, like a long-distance runner aching in his bones for the final stretch, through those last words. Rosalie's accusation made me work faster. As I read I felt Francine's presence ghosting around me. My sense of hurt and resentment was still a constant accomplice but I also felt a kind of spiritual companionship with her. It was undeniable that we were still on the same intellectual journey, that we were somehow in the same boat, even if she had decided to dive off.

As I read those last pages it was perversely comforting to think of her voice reacting to some of the insights here. When M Ageyev's *Novel With Cocaine* was mentioned I could almost hear her. Reminding me that the mysterious Ageyev submitted the novel to a publisher before vanishing himself. She reminded me that the book became a huge success in his absence. I could almost hear her telling me this was evidence that Valdez had planned a disappearance. I thought of the pointed references to Frances Farmer and James Dean. Surely they referenced the appeal of dying young? Francine's voice again spoke in my mind. 'But he wasn't young,' she says. 'Which leaves only one theory. Valdez was planning to vanish.'

I raced through the final pages. I could feel their physical thinness in my fingers. The pages were vanishing. It was like we were running out of tissue. Running out of him. I braced myself for the possibility there would be no answer at the end. But to my surprise, on the penultimate page I found a note:

No readings of my writing. Only flowers and music. My granddaughter, Velasco, and the women I've loved – that is all.

Besides a couple of poems – fractured to the point of illegibility, that was it.

I closed the last cover, leant back and took a deep breath. I exhaled, and imagined it spreading in the air before me.

It was painful knowing there was no answer, no final reckoning. Was that last missive a suicide note? If so, why was it not clearer? Why did it feel so slight? I hung my head.

I looked out at the sea. I watched the surf rise into what seemed like a huge wave, only for it to draw near, dissipate and wash over the feet of children on the shore. There may have been a sense that a huge revelation was to come but that didn't mean it would. Another wave came; the content of it bristling as white foam to its crest. When it broke, its dissolving only seemed absolute because of the peak of that bristling.

I placed my hands behind my head. I asked myself if, when it came to people, there was a final answer? There are thoughts, and there are decisions made. There is ignorance of what would have happened if alternatives were chosen. There are urgencies that people strive for. But what is at the end of them?

Driven by frustration, I moved upstairs into Velasco's office and tore open the first diary. I felt Rosalie bristle from somewhere in the house, tracking my movements. My sense of futility and rage had finally made me ready for whatever Velasco had to reveal, however dark. I knew that Rosalie was not questioning me because more than anything she did not want me to stop.

Having been in the company of a freewheeling mind for the past few days, I was curious to enter Velasco's mindset. I was hoping for schedules of encounters with women, itineraries. I was hoping for hard facts. I was also hoping for insights into a self-flagellating mind. To my chagrin I soon realised Velasco's diaries would be none of those things.

He wrote in sloping, almost illegible Spanish. The fact that I needed Rosalie to comprehend them felt like a sickening irony. I had somehow thought Velasco would use his friend's trick of writing in English. Rosalie must have known I could not read these books? Did she need someone to force her to open them?

I went downstairs. She was organising Valdez's books, with her back to me.

'I need your help. His diaries are in Spanish.'

She didn't turn.

'I can't do it without you,' I said.

She turned and looked at me, and opened her hands. 'So now you know how it feels,' she said.

With a grim look, she led me upstairs. Moments later we were back in the office as she stood over her legacy. Sat at the desk, I opened my notebook. I detected in her tensed frame an emboldened state. She was twitching. She was about to face her past, and she knew that this mattered.

The sense of anti-climax began to rise. Those diaries read more like sections of an unpublished autobiography than private reflections. Rosalie read them as she walked around the room. She paced with the disaffected tone of a historian, rather than that of a psychologically scarred granddaughter.

Velasco opened by describing his childhood – including his parents' financial struggles, his father's emotional distance, and his relocation during the Second World War. As Rosalie read his descriptions of the acute homesickness he felt she slowed his words down, as if trying to savour the emotion in them.

In later pages Velasco described flourishing in the world of academia. I wondered if Rosalie and I were supposed to take comfort in his brief childhood pain? Was that the only penance we would find here? Rosalie sat on the table while I took notes, looking up at her. Velasco had a constant need to impress upon the reader how exciting his work life was, how rewarding he found his relationship with Valdez, and how loved he felt at the university. I leant closer to her as she finished the second volume and began the third. Seeing Velasco's granddaughter ventriloquise for him felt bizarre. I was attracted to her intensity, but at the same time repulsed by the hints of Velasco that I could detect in her. As the day wore on Rosalie became synonymous with Velasco – she was not just his mouthpiece. Her words sped up when she read about his personal life. I wondered if she still felt an investment – even a love – for him that contradicted her earlier condemnation, and her fears. We were being drawn into his perspective and down its plughole. By being attracted to her, was I being drawn into his moral chasm?

One passage described how Velasco took any opportunity to help the less fortunate. He wrote of 'taking various women under his wing and mentoring them'. At this point Rosalie stopped, as if checking herself, and she looked down at me. The pained demeanour from the roof terrace had returned. 'I feel sick,' she said.

'We've got to keep going.'

She nodded. 'You're right.'

There was some hint at how helping people came with its own challenges, and then we were back to the linguistic slideshow of his various successes. We were back to how he found international travel fabulous, and to how his conferences and seminars were great fun. As Rosalie stacked emptied diaries behind her I realised she was running out of pages, and there were few notes on my page.

She stopped reading.

'What is it?' I asked.

She looked at the floor. 'During the years his abuse was at its worst he kept no diaries.'

'Did he destroy them? Or keep some other trophies?' I asked, picking discarded volumes off the table.

I flicked through them. The flowing writing suggested a life of leisure and ease. I looked for something else – sketches or pictures. Valdez had made me come to expect collages, annotations. The multimedia expressions of a reflexive mind. But here was nothing. The only addition to the entries was on the back page of one diary. A list of what appeared to be initials.

'Look at this,' I said. 'Could these lists record the women he thought of as conquests?'

She let the diary fall to her lap. 'That would be a very male thing to do.'

'What do you mean?'

'My ex kept nude photos of all his exes. He had folders for each of them. When I told him to delete them, he said: 'They're mine.'

'That's awful.'

She picked up the diary. 'Are you telling me you're so different?'

I thought of Lily. Of the exchanged glance between the taxi driver and I. Had his eyes judged what I was not doing – or doing? Something lurched in my stomach.

'Keep reading,' I said.

As she skipped through the final diary the mentions of Valdez were perfunctory. Velasco's need to relay a sense of pleasure, reward and achievement became pulverising. Rosalie's voice was deadened when she said: 'This is the final page.' The entry contained an anecdote about an honorary dinner where Velasco's long career was celebrated. She read it out, and then snapped the book shut.

'That is it,' she said.

I exhaled. 'The end of the line,' I answered.

I felt something collapse inside me. It was crushing to hear that Velasco had not suffered, but it was also a relief that Rosalie hadn't been mentioned. 'How do you feel?' I ask.

I don't know,' she said, folding her arms. 'You?'

I hated not having the answers Francine craved. But the fact that I was making it about me felt too perverse to admit.

Looking up at Rosalie, I found it impossible to read her expression. I realised then that reading her grandfather's diaries had altered her. The composition of elegance and dread that I had associated with her now had a third colour mixed in – that of resolution. She could decide what she thought now, and make her own verdict. As there was no more evidence to reveal.

19

We made dinner in her kitchen. The brief nap had made me feel like a new man. It had been a short, dreamless sleep in which I'd rejuvenated myself. As we chopped vegetables Rosalie kept her back to me. I wondered what historical battles were being expressed through the tension in her shoulders; the only part of her I could read. The black cardigan dampened any emanating mood.

That evening, Rosalie and I picked at salads on the outside patio. She pushed food around on her plate. 'Nothing incriminating, then,' she said.

I noticed that her blue dress ended in a collar that looked as if it might choke her. I felt too hollow to assist with her disappointment. 'It was not exactly the journey into a heart of darkness I had feared. Or that I had wanted.'

We discussed Velasco's pages; so full of celebration and so bereft of guilt and trauma. Pages in which his childhood pain and the death of his wife were the only emotional flashpoints. Even those had just been dark threads woven into a bright tapestry. The accusations of harassment had not warranted a single mention. 'It seems that even in his own mind there was no toll for his actions,' I said. 'It's bizarre.'

'Bizarre?'

'I ended up persuading myself that his childhood problems were some kind of karma for all the abuse he doled out in his later life. Given his sudden death I could see no other punishment he had to suffer.'

Rosalie took a deep sip of wine, and leant back. 'Hmm,' she said.

'What?' I asked.

She tucked locks of hair over her ear. There was a timidity to her smile that I found appealing.

'If even in his own diary a man can't admit any troubles, what do you think that might say?' she asked.

'I don't know.'

She spooned out salad. 'I think it suggests it was all too big for him to even contemplate.'

She looked out at the sea: to the thick bars of white on a distant ocean, that were advancing towards a gold shore. 'I've been thinking about this a lot over the past few days,' she said. 'Being holed up with these diaries has given me a really good chance to play it all out in my mind. Valdez, Velasco; who they really were. What happened to them.'

'And what have you decided?'

She closed her eyes for a moment. When she opened them the glacial intensity of their green unnerved me.

'With Valdez, you were hoping to find out where he went. But you found ambiguity. So the idea that someone can be found in their possessions is flawed.'

'Okay.'

'Valdez is in his work as much as he is anywhere. That is, in every respect – but not at all. He didn't find himself, but he spent a lifetime looking. So the idea that we could find him in those remains was wrong.'

I found myself nodding. 'And Velasco?'

She leant forward.

'All I learnt from those diaries was that he could not face what he had done.'

'We found no evidence of that.'

'Yes, we did,' she said, with a sympathetic smile.

I laid down my knife.

'Where?'

'We found huge evidence that he *could* not face what he had done. That he couldn't even *start* to.'

'Is it possible he had a happy life despite making other people's lives so unhappy?'

She shook her head.

'I've considered that question a great deal. I think that is a conclusion people come to when they can't face their own inadequacies, when they're stuck at some internal waystation between them. He spent a lot of time using words to create a huge fence around his unhappiness. I got a sense of his misery precisely because it was never mentioned,' she said.

'I can't help but feel disappointed.'

Her expression hardened. 'That's because those words weren't meant for you. They were meant for him. You went in with a certain premise and thought you'd find evidence for it. You went into someone else's narrative, and tried to make it your own.'

I thought of Francine. She was convinced she had found evidence of something being about to happen between Maria and I. As her premise had felt firm she had presumed the evidence was too. Having spent time with Maria since then I had evidence she was incorrect. But that hadn't changed Francine's mind, because she hadn't been open to what was there.

'I think I'm with you,' I said.

'Our sense of meaning comes from ourselves,' Rosalie added. 'So if yours doesn't work for you, change it.' Her expression lifted. 'Right now.'

'You make it sound easy.'

She pressed the tips of her fingers together. 'Velasco never did find a sense of meaning about the world. He couldn't even accurately report what had happened in his own life. He left all the hard parts out! Even when talking to himself. That is not evidence he was happy. That is evidence he was unhappy.'

'Yeah. But he wasn't punished, was he?'

'His punishment was in not knowing what he could have done with his life. If he had faced up to the fact that actions have consequences, he might have moved forward.'

19

'So are you saying that despite the self-congratulatory journals, the lavish lifestyle, and the sudden death keeping him from prison, he had a miserable life?'

She leant back, and considered the sea. It looked calm for once. Static, even. 'Maybe. Even if he didn't know it,' she said. 'But what I do know is that it isn't my business to know.'

20

In my room that night, I turned on my phone to find it full of messages. With increasing irritation Maria was asking me what I had found. Were the diaries even his? Had I had a problem translating them?

As I was texting my reply Rosalie tapped on the door.

'Yeah?'

She opened the door, and I saw she was holding two of Velasco's little red books. 'What is it?' I asked.

She looked taken aback by my tone as she opened a book at its rear sleeve. 'The initials at the back of this diary. I think they match the names of the victims and the order he … met them.'

'So?'

She stepped into the room, and seemed shocked by the state of it. I realised I had been living like an animal, my figure at night framed by messy clothes, resembling some dirty aura.

'These are diaries, Jude. They offer a time frame for a year. Presumably, any notes in them relate to a given year.'

She handed me the book. I looked again at the initials. The first one was E.S. I thought back to Barcelona.

'Emilie Sierra,' I said. 'I met her.'

The memory of those trapped expressions, that row of uneasy companionship, brought with it details of the press report I'd read about her.

'Emilie claims she was abused seven years ago.' I looked at the year on the front of the diary. 'Christ,' I said. 'It matches.'

'Oh my god,' Rosalie said, clasping her hand to her mouth.

'Do you think this would be enough to convince a jury?'

Her eyes were fixed on the page, as if she couldn't believe what she was holding. 'Perhaps,' she said. 'If he had claimed to have never met her – it could.'

I looked back at my phone.

'At least I have something to text Maria. Even if it probably is too late,' I said.

21

It was two hours later when Maria replied. I was lying in the dark, listening to the roar of distant waves from one side of the house, and passing traffic from the other. My phone throbbed on the pillow next to me, lighting the gloom in an amber dome.

I've spoken to Joan Suarez. She thinks this evidence could be huge.

Moments later, another text.

Can you send us screen shots of the initials and the cover right away?

I was starting to type my response when a third message came through from her.

On behalf of all of us over here. Thank you.

I tapped at the screen in the dark. How could something covered in dust, in another continent, be of such impactful use to so many?

It was Rosalie who found it.

22

The following morning, over breakfast, Rosalie suggested I stay another day in Casablanca. We agreed on the importance of purging all this information before returning back to our lives. No matter how dark the subject matter under consideration it felt better to be talking about that than returning to the hollowness of my life in England. Out here, at least I'd had a mission. However futile it had often seemed.

As we ate Rosalie insisted she show me some of the sights. 'We have to visit the Hassan Mosque. I think you in particular might find it interesting.'

'How so?'

The green in her eyes came alive. 'For a start it's this enormous palace, set out on a limb, over the ocean,' she said.

I was reminded of Velasco's claim that Valdez had thrown himself from a cliff, into the North Atlantic. I wondered if, at the Mosque, I would be looking out at an ocean that contained him?

'And we have to have lunch at Rick's Café.'

'That's the place from that film – Casablanca?'

She nodded. 'The last time Valdez was discharged the two of them went for a meal there.'

My ears pricked up. I had considered it indelicate to tell her of my confrontation with her grandfather. But the possible significance of Rick's Café and the Mosque made doing so now seem a necessity.

'Time to be a tourist, Jude,' she said, puzzling over my expression. 'But do me a favour – tidy yourself up.'

As we settled amongst the flowing white pillars and Arabic lamps at Rick's Café, I felt myself relax. While Rosalie ordered wine and terrines in fluid French I looked below me, at the seating area underneath. I wondered who else had sat at our table, on the encircling balcony. It allowed you to watch others without them seeing you. It struck me as the perfect place for a writer to eat.

'What's on your mind?' she asked. Her leopard print coat evoked, to me, the stylish women of European cities. When I thought of the disgraced aristocrats and exiled diplomats of the Casablanca film her style blended with it. It was as if we were dining with ghosts.

'I'm thinking back to when I first got that letter. The award from Valdez. I'm wondering if I have really got anywhere since then.'

I thought of Francine.

'You finished off Valdez's collection. You helped bring Velasco to justice – with me.'

'I think you deserve more credit.'

Her smile was prim. She was enjoying the role that this place had cast her in, with its smothered echoes of ruined ages. Even then, people were running away from their pasts and trying to find themselves. History had enshrined them – not least in the glass posters around us. But the people in those frames had been in flux then as well. 'Well, who am I to argue?' she said. 'Maria thinks that what we found could save the whole legal case.'

'It could lead to you having to sell your family home.'

She placed her hand on top of mine. The warmth of it made me tingle.

'Fine by me,' she said. 'It might look solid but sometimes old things … I don't know. Built with lies, and all that. Best destroyed.'

The wine arrived. An oaky, dark red. The taste of it relaxed some conflicting thoughts in my mind. I had spent so long loathing Velasco and now his granddaughter was becoming my greatest reason to hope. What would he think if the two of us ended up together? What if we ended up having children? Would they have something méchant in their blood? The possibility, however remote, was confronting me with how futile it was to loathe anyone.

As I sipped I had the strange sensation that my consciousness was sliding into other realms. Was Velasco here somehow? In his granddaughter I knew he was present, and in the incantatory thoughts Rosalie and I shared by visiting this place. But was he here in another respect?

'I feel good about what we found,' I said. 'Even if we couldn't answer what happened to Valdez. I think in the end it was the sense of meaning you gave me about it all that felt most significant.'

'I'm glad,' she said. 'It has been comforting for me, too.'

Her fingers weaved into mine. I experienced a swinging hit of pleasure. Her blonde hair had stuck to the leopard print fabric of her lapel. I felt as if we were protagonists in a tragic drama.

The heat from the afternoon sun was still prickling my arms. Earlier we had picked our way amongst the marble floors and expansive interiors of the Mosque. There was a moment when I looked through the small, dust-covered windows of the Mosque out at the ocean, and questioned if Valdez was out there somewhere.

'What's on your mind?' she asked.

'I spoke to your grandfather. Not long before he died,' I said.

'How?'

I told her about Maria's invite, and the atmosphere I had found at the courthouse. I recalled that snatched argument in the bathroom, where so much was revealed. The deeper I went into the story the further she sat back in her chair.

'What is it?' I asked.

'This is the table where the two of them sat on the day Valdez was discharged. They had lunch here. The last time I visited a waiter came over and told me that. He offered me his sympathies.'

'Is that why you brought me here?'

'I suppose so. I suppose for me—' she looked up at an overhead lamp. 'For me, this table is where the trail ends. It seemed right to bring you here.'

'That's true. We can pursue people who are gone as much as we like. But at the end all we can do is stand at the end of the trail and look around us.'

'True.' She lowered her eyes.

'Are you angry with me? I held off telling you what happened at the court because—'

'Why?'

'I don't know. Sensitivity. I thought it might colour anything we found out here.'

'Well, it does.'

She cradled her fingers together.

'How?'

She looked over the side. Beneath us a waiter in a Fez was offering champagne to an elderly couple. The woman's diamonds glinted in a piercing ray. 'Well, I don't know how significant this is. But the timeline Velasco gave you in the courthouse fits.'

'In what way?'

'The last time Valdez was seen was just after he met my grandfather. Here.'

'I accused your grandfather of killing Valdez.'

Her expression didn't move. 'And what did he say to that?'

'He said I didn't want to accept that he had told me the truth. He said I preferred my own account and the mystery – and money – that came with it.'

She tucked a lock of hair behind her ear. The light caught her cheekbone. For a moment she looked like a film star, and I suspected she knew that.

'So is that why he didn't tell people the truth? Money?'

I nodded. 'Apparently.'

She sipped her wine. 'So this table is not where the trail ends. It ends on a cliff top ... somewhere.'

Play It Again Sam oozed through the speakers. 'The waiters must get sick of that song,' I said.

Her frown furrowed. 'You know the significance of Casablanca? In the film?'

'Tell me.'

'It is the place everyone gets stuck at. The place everyone wants to escape.'

'Like the end of the trail,' I said.

'So here we are.' She raised her glass in a mock toast. 'They had to be somewhere, and they ended up here. I suppose we have to be somewhere, and here we are here.'

'Here we are,' I echoed.

I looked around, at the turn of the century lamps, the stills from the film captured in thick glass.

'At least we get to leave. If we want to.'

'True. So what's next for you?' I asked.

Her mouth twisted into a smile. 'I've got into King's College London. To do a PhD in music.'

'I didn't know you played.'

She laughed. 'In a sense there's quite a lot we don't know about each other.'

'Don't start that,' I said.

She smiled. 'You must think it bizarre. You came out to find a monster. Yet here you are with his granddaughter...'

'Getting on better than I thought we would,' I said.

She sipped her wine. The red seemed to bloom in her cheeks. 'I must admit, when I first met you I wasn't entirely sure about you. But your determination to get to the heart of the matter... '

'What about it?'

'I admired it. And it's really helped me.'

'Well, you've helped me as well.'

'In what way?' She suspended her glass between her fingers. The surface of the liquid caught the light. For a moment I caught an image of my smiling face on it. 'You are going to write this story when you get home,' she said. 'It's your next book.'

'Maybe. It doesn't feel like it has quite ended yet.' I thought of what Lily said. 'I can't write it until I know what it is.'

'That's not true. You can write it and it can even get published, and that's no guarantee anyone knows what it is. You're starting a conversation: a narrative. That's all we can do.'

'I suppose you're right. Still; I'd like to know what I'm dealing with.'

There was something flickering in her eyes. I realised that over the last few days I had barely thought of Francine. 'Are you talking about the story, or about you and I?' she asked.

I met her eye. I was embarrassed by the smile I couldn't hide. 'I don't know,' I said.

Something was being held back in her gaze. A waiter in a Fez, uncorking champagne, distracted me. *Play It Again, Sam* was whirring on the jukebox yet again. The Chinese diners behind us burst into simultaneous laughter. It seemed an appropriate response. There was no final answer and no final resolution. Just loose ends, questions people were tired of asking, and people who had once walked on the same floors as us. People who breathed the same air and absorbed the same light, but who were now gone. Leaving behind a sense of absurdity and the sound of laughter that echoed through the ages.

23

As I entered the glass walls of Andrea's third floor office, she waved me towards a seat. I marvelled at how much us writers vaunted the validation of gatekeepers like her, who waved through life-shaping projects on a whim. Did what you were doing echo where they thought the world of publishing was heading? If so, come on through. Does your artistic expression seem too out of synch with what happened to just commercially succeed? Then back into the cold you go. As I touched the arms of her armchair I said to myself, 'This validation is temporary.'

There was something mercurial about her expression that had so often settled into a smile of stifled sadism. But the weather had blown her in a different direction today. Usually, her blend of grunge sweaters and expensive Fendi cardigans seemed all part of an impenetrable façade, and one that did not validate my existence. Never once had she invited me to sit down, wearing a look of disdain when I did, as if I was muddying the furniture. But today, her dishevelled, thick dark hair framed a round face with a smile that seemed more pliant.

'There's something here,' she said, tapping the pages with a smile weak enough that I might have been imagining it.

I had been trying not to worry about my agent's reaction to the story. I had felt as if all the creative blockages holding me back had dissolved in the two months since I had returned from Morocco. I had almost forgotten what it was like to wait for a verdict on a new novel. That inflated sense of optimism, followed by a gritty response that, on some level, you already knew.

London flickered in the late afternoon sun behind her, and the heat from it soothed me as I sat back in the chair.

As she leant forward I detected her gauging my reaction. Her tight red dress with pink patterns looked new; she kept readjusting it as if disappointed in how it fell on her. I took in the grey-blue of her eyes. With her blend of American ambition and English studiousness Andrea had a tendency to embolden and unnerve me at the same time.

'I know a few publishers who might well respond to this story. When can you have a whole draft finished?'

'Soon,' I said. 'Very soon.'

She pointed a painted finger at me. 'Exactly what I wanted to hear.'

My eyes drifted over her shoulder, to the wall of her clients. It struck me as odd that I was looking for Francine's face, when mine had never graced the wall. When I had signed to her I had fostered dreams of being featured alongside authors of her I admired, but when I emailed a photo I'd elicited only a tart 'let's see, shall we?' in response to it. There were a few pasty, self-regarding grins on there that I didn't recognise. I had always marvelled at the way the publishing world represented humans – with their messy inner worlds and loose ends – as sophisticates. In their promotional photos, they always suggested writers as lacking the animalism their writing portrayed. To me, authors' work was the result of the agitation of an oyster, gradually accumulating something in its shell through sheer irritation and agitation. Creating matter of value only to those ready to deem it of value.

'Any interesting new clients on the books?' I asked, unable to meet her eye. I had still not heard another word from – or about – Francine. At times it had been difficult not to interpret her silence as part of a conspiracy that fate had against me.

Andrea's eyes considered my shoes. 'Not since I signed you and Francine,' she said.

She cocked her head to one side. I hadn't noticed before how strong her jaw was, how hard her bob looked in a certain light.

'Why don't you get in touch with her?' she asked.

I tried to hide a grimace. So the financial implication of my heartbreak had sunk in. 'Because she vanished without saying a word to me.'

Andrea's bemusement was agitating me.

'Still – you could drop her a line. Say 'I don't like how things ended. Maybe we should meet?''

'I could do,' I said. 'But I think the ball is in her court.'

She scratched her head.

'Does she know about this book?' she asked. 'About where you went, what you found out?'

'Not unless you've told her.'

Andrea stood up, and moved over to the window. 'Two former friends, and lovers, working on the same story. Yet neither of you can bring yourself to pick up the phone. How ridiculous. You both have so much to gain from talking. Do you even realise the holes you are making in yourself by both refusing to?'

She considered the slow crawl of a distant airplane. Its slipstream a long, thin wound in the sky.

'I get the picture,' she said. 'It's a staring contest between two people, both too outraged to back down. And yes, I think she could've handled it better.'

Her mild condemnation of Francine was far worse that her refusing to discuss it; I felt belittled. 'Perhaps,' I said, 'giving someone space allows them to properly understand what they've let go of. They can't do that except on their own.'

She furrowed her brow. I realised that any seeming advice she'd been offering hadn't been empathic, but studied lines from someone versed in how the world communicated. My thin attempt to engage with her on a sincere level was bound to cause bafflement. I chided myself for being naïve enough to try to talk to her on that level.

I remembered that in all the time I'd known Andrea she'd always kept me on the back foot. She'd often acted as if suggestions I made might be the final straw, even if they had turned out to be well-founded. As if I was somehow unworthy of her respect, that I came up short in comparison to her other clients. It had been a useful position for an agent to keep their client in. It meant that whatever position she took in any situation (and I'd realised her positions were more stances taken in response to where the wind was blowing than as a result of any sincere approach) she did not have to acknowledge how it contradicted previous stances she'd taken.

I felt my patience run dry. I had seen through her persona and I did not like what I had seen. I was not sure what would come next in life but it would involve keeping people like her as distant from me – from my inner world – as possible. All she had was more vague, allusive answers when some comforting information would have made life so much more tolerable. Francine was now just another vanished person in my life, a blank template. The fact that she was one who had been more present, more physical than any of the other figures I concerned myself with just made the situation all the more bizarre.

Andrea turned and faced me. I wondered if there was a slight smile on her lips as she said, 'You do realise what your book will do, don't you? It'll finish hers.'

'Really?'

A very Andrea statement. The world, by implication, depicted as a place in which every scintilla of advantage in terms of finances or attention was to be jealously contested. I had no interest in harming Francine; I wanted us all to thrive. But I was in the midst of a game, and making more statements she probably did not comprehend would only make her play more aggressively.

'Of course. I can't take on one book stating Valdez is alive while another suggests he checked out.'

'The thought hadn't occurred to me.'

23

Her smile was broad now, unashamed. 'I know what you're thinking. If she'd have kept a grip on her jealousy she'd still have a piece of the action.'

She liked this. The 'artists' she had to deal with, who lived in a world of feeling she could not relate to, were being punished for their nature.

I dug deep. I was surprised at what I found. 'If she gets in touch I'll share whatever answers I might have found. But she'll have to swallow her pride. If she...' I tried to find the right words, without relapsing into obvious self-pity. 'She'll have to take some responsibility for the mess she left me with.'

Andrea's expression flickered between the Machiavellian, the acquiescing, and then the accepting. 'She is probably struggling quite a lot, you know. For what it's worth, I think the two of you should join forces. You'll be so strong if you can.'

Yes, I thought, and something healing between us only being a concern of yours when it's so glaringly obvious it'll benefit you that your mean-spiritedness is finally overcome.

'I'd be happy to.'

I thought of the diaries. Of how unknowable Valdez and Velasco had turned out to be. I wondered if Rosalie had read her grandfather's words to me as they were, or if she had in any way curated them for me. Had she curated what he had curated? Given how elusive those people had proven how could I expect to understand Francine?

I felt comforted by what I had found out in Casablanca. It might have been inconclusive, but it was *something*. I knew that much because I had found, in those pages, Valdez to be distinct from the image I had in my mind. I had at least learnt something. I had learnt not to build conclusions about people in your mind, but to allow them to be in flux.

Andrea seemed to be suppressing a smile. 'You mean that?'

'Of course I do,' I said. 'But it wouldn't be easy to explain it all. Rosalie and I came to some conclusions about Valdez and Velasco that are far from comfortable.'

'Rosalie and I, eh?' Her accent had become Texan. She walked over to me, and put a hand on my shoulder.

'Yes,' I said. 'Rosalie and I.'

'I'll pass your offer onto Francine. But she'll need to not fly off the handle at any mentions of this Rosalie.'

I wasn't sure what to make of the remark. But I felt relieved someone was now interested in ending the impasse. 'Okay,' I said.

'Changing the subject – I take it you've heard the news? After all those delays, the women are going to be awarded significant damages. Those initials you both found in that diary turned out to be key.'

I exhaled. 'When did you hear this?'

'While you were on your way in.'

I tried to absorb the information. Andrea shook her head, and for once I sensed genuine bitterness. 'You know what they say – justice delayed is justice denied. I hear a lot of these women are distraught that Velasco will never be behind bars.'

I stood up. 'I think he paid in his own way.'

'What do you mean?'

I thought of Rosalie's words on the terrace, and wished she was here to explain it.

'Well, I'll save it for the book,' I said, buttoning my coat.

24

It was autumn, and as I passed through the square below Andrea's office I saw a crescent of rich brown leaves hugging the edge of the green. I pulled my collar up, and wondered how I was supposed to process all the feelings I had. How I could twist together the disparate strands of my life into a single strand. I felt at once resolved, unsure, betrayed and grateful.

Rosalie was sat, in a black jacket with a white fur collar, on a bench at the end of the park. Her white-blonde hair combined with the trimming to add the regal touch that was starting to define her. As I walked towards her she flicked through a book that had a large musical note on the cover. When she saw me I realised the season agreed with her solemn, almost meditative air. She seemed compact within her clothes, snug. A universe shrink-wrapped in fine skin – impenetrable.

'How did it go?' she asked.

I settled down beside her, and relayed the story. I felt something inside me loosen. I knew I could tell her what was on my mind without fear of a sharp and painful reaction. There was some comfort in knowing that.

As I surveyed the park I wondered when the leaves had turned. It made me think of all the multiple states of minds I could adopt, all the different meanings I could cultivate. I felt free, and yet more settled than I had done in years.

Rosalie chatted about her day; about how another student had expressed envy for her musical ability. It was good to see her step out of her family's shadow and into the light thrown by her talent.

I followed her eyes. She traced a walker coming through the path that wound past us. Something seemed to tingle in Rosalie's expression. I followed her gaze to see Francine, in a long beige mackintosh. Looking right at me as she walked in my direction.

I looked back at her. Rosalie looked at me.

'Who's that?' she asked.

I realised I was holding Francine's gaze and that she was holding mine. For those fleeting seconds, a delicate wager was taking place. In my mind I thought 'Speak to me if you want to, and then I'll speak back.'

Her hair was longer; darker. As her path drew her closer to me I saw in her eyes a delicate flicker. A flash of something I recognised all too well; a wager being settled. Her gazes snapped from me, to Rosalie and then back at me. I saw a mixture of anger, shame and defiance. I inhaled.

'Francine,' I said.

'Jude,' she answered.

Her face looked a little gaunt, a little red.

As her path drew her closer I turned to Rosalie. 'This is Velasco's granddaughter, Rosalie.'

Francine kept walking, and the sinking feeling in my stomach told me she was going to move right past us.

'You've probably learnt about her, in the course of writing your book,' I said. My words hung in the still air, and I judged their tone.

Francine looked at Rosalie.

'Good to meet you,' she said.

Rosalie bunched up on the bench. 'Join us for a minute,' she said. 'I think you might be interested in what we found.'

Francine looked at me. 'Jude?'

'Fine by me,' I said.

Francine smiled as she sat next to Rosalie. It was bizarre – the three of us huddled up on one bench.

'I found a few things that might be of interest to you, too,' she said, her breath forming in the air.

Rosalie looked between the two of us. 'Where do we start?' she asked.

I realised then that there was going to be no moment of communion. We were all so different to start with, and our experiences had only taken us further apart. In time, Francine would tell me that she regretted every day tearing herself out of my life like she did, and that she woke up each morning and asked herself why she had done that. In time, she would tell me it had made her feel as if she were living someone else's life. She would relate with sadness that she knew that even telling me that, and giving me all she had in terms of an explanation, with all the vulnerability that entailed, would never walk her and I back across that bridge to being connected with one another. I had craved answers for a while, but would such insights help in the last reckoning?

There had even been times when the inexplicably destructive choices of others had tempted me to wish something on them, but what really was the point of that? I had gone far down the path of that wish, and still not had it validated. Some people, as I'd seen, led lives that were one long act of implosion and it was not for others looking on to seek comfort in that.

When I panned back from that scene I saw all of us at most as mere foot soldiers in the battle of life. At the least, mere dust being ground somewhere underneath them. Reality, it seemed to me, was the vast event sprawling around it all. Not a war at all, but a vibrant being which we only flickered into contact with, at most.

I realised that there is no day of reckoning, no final day in which it all works out. In retrospectives of our lives it's how we made others feel and how, without obstacle, we review our endeavours to that end which is what matters.

There is simply the arc of your life, the heft of everything you've gathered, and how you feel about it.

When all is said and done, that is it.

Author biography

Guy Mankowski was the singer in the band Alba Nova. He trained as an assistant psychologist at The Royal Hospital for neuro-disability in London. His debut novel, *The Intimates*, was a recommended title by New Writing North. His second novel, *Letters from Yelena,* was researched in the world of Russian ballet and was awarded an Arts Council literature grant. The novel was adapted for the stage by the choreographer Dora Frankel and used in GCSE training material by Osiris Educational. His third novel, *How I Left the National Grid*, was written as part of his PhD at Northumbria University. *An Honest Deceit* was a New Writing North Read regional title, and released on Audible. *Dead Rock Stars* was published by Darkstroke in 2020. His first work of non-fiction was *Albion's Secret History: Snapshots of England's Pop Rebels and Outsiders* (Zer0 Books) for which he interviewed key figures in English music, including Gary Numan.

He's a full-time lecturer at Lincoln University. His TEDx talk on his experience of opening Kristen Pfaff's unseen archive for a forthcoming biography (written with her brother, Jason Pfaff) was entitled *Lived Through This: Kristen Pfaff's Hidden Archive and Influence.*

Guy Mankowski
Blogspot: http://www.guymankowski.blogspot.com
Instagram: @guymankowski
X: @Gmankow
Facebook: @guymankowskiauthor

Book Club Questions

- What role does the media play in exposing corrupt individuals and how has this evolved over the years?
- To what extent do institutions protect corrupt individuals and how might this occur?
- 'Institutional closure' is a term sometimes used to describe how certain professions protect their own, at the expense of justice. To what extent is this an increasing issue? And if so, why?
- The book discusses contemporary issues about masculinity with reference to the #MeToo movement. What role do men play as allies in this issue?
- The book also focuses on inter-generational inequality. To what extent are millennials having to seek redress for economic disparity between generations? If there is an inter-generational redress required is this normal, or unprecedented?
- In the novel Kimberley and Jude are facing similar economic issues. Is this merely due to their line of work or is there something here about the competition between millennials having intensified due to increasing economic insecurity in that generation?
- In 2023 there was huge controversy over Luis Rubiales, head of the Spanish FA, kissing Jenni Hermoso at the award ceremony when her team won the World Cup, without Hermoso's permission. Rubiales had originally doubled down and was backed by the Spanish FA before being forced to quit. What do you think links this case, and the Velasco case described in the book?

FICTION

Put simply, we publish great stories. Whether it's literary or popular, a gentle tale or a pulsating thriller, the connecting theme in all Roundfire fiction titles is that once you pick them up you won't want to put them down.
If you have enjoyed this book, why not tell other readers by posting a review on your preferred book site.

The Cause
Roderick Vincent
The second American Revolution will be a
fire lit from an internal spark.
Paperback: 978-1-78279-763-0 ebook: 978-1-78279-762-3

Don't Drink and Fly
The Story of Bernice O'Hanlon: Part One
Cathie Devitt
Bernice is a witch living in Glasgow. She loses her way
in her life and wanders off the beaten track looking for the
garden of enlightenment.
Paperback: 978-1-78279-016-7 ebook: 978-1-78279-015-0

Gag
Melissa Unger
One rainy afternoon in a Brooklyn diner, Peter Howland
punctures an egg with his fork. Repulsed, Peter pushes
the plate away and never eats again.
Paperback: 978-1-78279-564-3 ebook: 978-1-78279-563-6

The Master Yeshua
The Undiscovered Gospel of Joseph
Joyce Luck
Jesus is not who you think he is. The year is 75 CE. Joseph
ben Jude is frail and ailing, but he has a prophecy to fulfil …
Paperback: 978-1-78279-974-0 ebook: 978-1-78279-975-7

On the Far Side, There's a Boy
Paula Coston
Martine Haslett, a thirty-something 1980s woman, plays hard
on the fringes of the London drag club scene until one night
which prompts her to sign up to a charity. She writes to a
young Sri Lankan boy, with consequences far and long.
Paperback: 978-1-78279-574-2 ebook: 978-1-78279-573-5

Tuareg
Alberto Vazquez-Figueroa
With over 5 million copies sold worldwide, *Tuareg* is a classic
adventure story from best-selling author Alberto Vazquez-
Figueroa, about honour, revenge and a clash of cultures.
Paperback: 978-1-84694-192-4

Readers of ebooks can buy or view any of these bestsellers by
clicking on the live link in the title. Most titles are published
in paperback and as an ebook. Paperbacks are available in
traditional bookshops. Both print and ebook formats are
available online.

Find more titles and sign up to our readers' newsletter at
www.collectiveinkbooks.com/fiction